Acquainted with **THE NIGHT**

A Novel by **HEINRICH BÖLL**

Acquainted with **THE NIGHT**

Translated by **RICHARD GRAVES**

Henry Holt and Company · *New York*

Acquainted with **THE NIGHT**

FRED

At closing time I went to the pay office to get my wages.
There was a long line of people standing at the pay
window and I had to wait for half an hour for my turn.
Then I handed in my ticket and saw the cashier give it
to a girl in a yellow blouse. She went to a heap of em-
ployees' pay cards, looked mine up, and gave my ticket
back to the cashier saying, "O.K.," and he counted out
the notes on the marble slab. I noticed how clean his
hands were. I checked his count and pushed my way
out of the crowd. Then I sat down at a little table near
the door, where I could put the money in an envelope
and send it, with a note, to my wife. On the table there

were some pink pay forms. I took one of these and wrote in pencil on the back, "I must see you tomorrow. I'll ring up before two o'clock." I stuck the paper in the envelope and pushed the notes in after it, licked the gum, hesitated, and then picked a ten-mark note out of the bundle and put it in my coat pocket. I also took the paper out and wrote a P.S. saying, "I have taken ten marks for myself. You shall have it back tomorrow. Kiss the children for me. Fred." The envelope wouldn't stick any more, so I went to an empty cashier's window. The girl behind the glass hatch got up and raised the pane. She was sallow and thin and wore a pink pullover in the neck of which she had pinned an artificial rose. I said to her, "Please give me a strip of sticking tape." She looked at me, hesitated a moment, tore off a strip from a brown roll, and handed it to me without a word. Then she pulled the glass down. I said, "Thanks," into the glass, went back to my table, stuck down the envelope, pulled on my cap, and left the office.

It was raining when I came out and stray leaves were sailing along the asphalt. I waited for a while by the office entrance until a Number 12 tram came round the corner, when I jumped on and rode as far as Tuckhoff Square. There were a great many people in the tram and a strong smell of wet clothes. At Tuckhoff Square I jumped off, without paying, into still heavier rain. I hurried for shelter under the canvas roof of a sausage booth, pushed my way to the counter and ordered a hot sausage and a cup of bouillon. I also bought myself a package of cigarettes out of the ten-mark note. As I was biting into my sausage, I looked into the mirror which covered the whole back of the booth. At first I did not recognize myself when I saw a haggard, gray face under a faded beret. Then I realized that I looked like one of the men who used to call at my mother's house and were never turned away. I used to be struck by the deadly disconsolateness of their faces, when, as a kid, I would sometimes open the door to them and bring them into our dim hall. Keeping a fearful eye on our coat pegs, I would call my mother anxiously, but when she came out of the kitchen, drying her hands on her apron, a strange and somehow disquieting light appeared on the faces of those unhappy creatures, who came to sell soap flakes, floor polish, razor blades, or shoe laces. The expression of joy on these gray faces which the mere sight of my mother evoked was somehow terrible. My mother was a good woman. She was incapable of turning anyone away from her door. She gave beggars bread, when we had any; money, when we had any; a cup of coffee to drink and, when there was nothing in the house, a drink of fresh water in a clean glass and the consolation of her friendly eyes. Round about our door-bell beggars and tramps had scratched their signs, and peddlers knew they had a chance of selling something to us, if only a pair of shoe laces on which my mother was ready to spend her last penny. My mother was no more cautious in her dealings with commercial travelers. She could not resist the faces of these hard-run citizens and was ready to sign contracts of sale, insurance policies, and any other sort of document. I remember, when

I lay in bed as a child in the evening, what it was like when my father came home. As soon as he got into the dining room the storm burst. But it was a sort of one-sided, phantom-slinging match, in which my mother hardly spoke a word. She was a silent woman. One of these men who came to our house wore a faded beret like the one I now wear. His name was Disch and, as I learned later, he was an ex-priest. He traveled in soap flakes.

While I was eating my sausage I realized, looking into the mirror, how like I was growing to this man Disch—the same faded beret, the same thin, gray face, the same disconsolate expression. Alongside my reflection I saw the faces of my neighbors, their mouths opened wide to bite into their sausages. I saw good hats, bad hats, and the wet heads of hatless customers, and the rosy face of the sausage woman moving up and down among them. She smiled cheerfully as she speared the hot sausages in their bath of sizzling lard, slapped mustard on cardboard plates, served lemonade, and handed out cigarettes and took the money for them with her pink, stubby fingers, and all the time the rain drummed on the roof of the tent.

And when I looked at my own face as I was taking a bite at my sausage, I saw my mouth open on the dark cavern of my throat, and in my eyes I saw the same expression of soft greediness that had shocked me in others. Our heads were lined up in a row, like puppets in a show, half veiled in the warm haze that rose from the frying pans. Shocked by what I saw, I pushed my

4

way out and ran through the rain into Mozart Street. A lot of people were waiting under the shop awnings for the rain to stop, and when I got to Wagner's workshop, I had to struggle through the crowd to reach the door and could hardly pull it open. It was a great relief to get inside and down the steps, and to smell the reek of leather rising to meet me. It smelled like sweaty old shoes, new leather, and tar, and I heard the old-fashioned stitching machine at work.

I passed two women waiting on a bench, opened the glass door, and was glad to see Wagner greet me with a smile. I have known him for thirty-five years. We used to live in an upper story which no longer exists, above what is now the cement roof of his shop, and I remember bringing him my mother's slippers when I was a child of five. The crucifix is still hanging on the wall behind his work stool and near it is the picture of St. Crispin, a gentle old man with a gray beard, holding an iron trivet in hands too well kept for a cobbler's.

I shook hands with Wagner. His mouth was full of nails, so he silently beckoned to me to sit down on the other stool, which I did. As I was taking the envelope out of my pocket, he pushed his tobacco pouch and some cigarette papers across the table. My own cigarette was still alight, so I thanked him and held out the envelope saying, "Perhaps . . ."

He took the nails out of his mouth, passed his finger over his raw lips to find out if there was still a nail sticking to them, and said, "Another message for your wife—dear me!"

He took the envelope from me, shook his head, and said, "It shall be attended to. I'll send my grandson over when he comes back from confession in"—he looked at the clock—"in half an hour."

"She wants it today, there's money inside," I said.

"Yes, I know."

I gave him my hand and went away. As I was going up the steps it occurred to me that I might have asked him for a loan. I hesitated for a moment and then climbed the last step and shouldered my way through the crowd into the street.

It was still raining when, five minutes later, I got out of the bus in Benekam Street. I ran along between the towering Gothic houses which had been propped up by the authorities as buildings of architectural interest. Through the burned-out gaps which had been windows I could see the gray sky. Only one of these houses is inhabited. I hurried under the porch, rang the bell, and waited.

The brown eyes of the servant girl regarded me with the same look of pity with which I used to gaze at my mother's clients whom I am so clearly beginning to resemble. She took my overcoat and beret, shook them out in front of the door, and said, "Goodness, you must be wet through!" I nodded, walked over to a looking glass, and passed my hands through my hair.

I asked, "Is Mrs. Beisem there?"

"No."

"I wonder if she has remembered that tomorrow is the first."

"I don't suppose so," said the girl. She took me into the living room, drew the table near the stove, and brought me a chair. But I remained standing with my back against the stove and looking at the clock which has been telling the time to the Beisem family for a hundred and fifty years. The room is full of old furniture and the windows still have their original Gothic glass.

The girl came in with a cup of coffee for me in one hand and leading young Alphonse by his braces with the other. Alphonse is the Beisems' boy to whom I have engaged myself to teach the rules of vulgar fractions. He is a healthy child with ruddy cheeks. His chief amusement is playing with chestnuts collected in the big garden of the Beisems' house and in the gardens of the neighboring uninhabited houses, and on fine days, when the windows were left open, I could see long chains of chestnuts hanging from tree to tree.

I clasped my coffee cup in my two hands and sipped its warmth into my body, repeating the while the rules of fractions to the healthy young face in front of me, knowing all the time that it was useless. The child is amiable but stupid—stupid as his parents and his brothers and sisters are. In fact, there is only one intelligent person in the house and that is the servant girl. Mr. Beisem deals in hides and scrap metal. He is a nice fellow, and often, when we meet and have a few minutes' talk, I have the absurd feeling that he envies me my profession as a switchboard operator. I have the impression that all his life he has suffered from the feeling that more is expected of him than he can perform. He is at the head of a big concern which requires both toughness and intelligence. He possesses neither. When we meet he questions me with such deep interest about the details of my trade that I am beginning to believe that he would prefer to spend his life shut up in a small telephone exchange as I do. He insists on knowing how I work at the switchboard and how I fix long-distance calls, and asks me about the jargon of our profession. The idea that I can listen in to any conversation gives him a childish pleasure. "Interesting," he keeps on saying, "How interesting!"

The hands of the clock crept slowly on. I made Alphonse repeat the rules, dictated exercises to him, and, waited, smoking, till he had finished doing them. Not a sound came from outside the house. Here, in the heart of the town, it is as quiet as in a tiny village in the middle of the steppes when the herds have been driven away to their summer pasture and only a few sick old women remain behind.

Meanwhile Alphonse continued doing his divisions, substituting the numerator for the denominator, when suddenly he looked up at me and said, "Clemens did well in Latin." I don't know if he noticed what a shock his words gave me. His remark immediately brought to my mind a picture of a pale-faced, thirteen-year-old boy and I remembered that he sits next to Alphonse in class.

"That is fine," I said wearily, "and you?"

"I did not do so well." His eyes looked doubtfully at my face, as if he was seeking something. I felt myself blushing, but almost instantly became indifferent to his feelings, for it seemed to me as if the faces of my wife and children, more than life-sized, were thrown on to my vision and I had to cover my face with my hands. "Get on with it," I said. "How do you multiply fractions by one another?" He repeated the rule quietly, looking at me as he did so, but I did not listen to him. I saw my children harnessed to the deadly routine of life, which begins when one first puts on one's satchel to go to school, and ends somewhere on an office stool. My mother saw me put my satchel on my back and go off to school every morning and now, every morning, Kate, my wife, sees our children doing just the same thing.

I went on aiming questions about the rules of fractions at the child's face and some of them came back to me correctly and the hour passed, albeit slowly, and I had earned two marks fifty. I dictated homework to the boy to prepare for the next lesson and drank up the last mouthful of cold coffee. Then I went out into the hall where I found the girl, who helped me on with my overcoat which she had dried in the kitchen. She gave me a smile. As I went out into the street I thought of her coarse, good-natured face and it occurred to me that I might have asked her for money. I hesitated for an instant and then turned up my coat collar, for it was still raining, and hurried to the bus stop which is by the Church of the Seven Sorrows of Mary.

Ten minutes later I was sitting in a kitchen, which smelled of vinegar, in a southern quarter of the town and a pale-faced girl with large yellowish eyes was repeating Latin phrases to me. Once the door of the neighboring room opened and a haggard woman's face with the same yellow eyes as the girl looked in and said, "Work hard, child, you know how difficult it is for me to send you to school and your lessons cost money."

The child did work hard and so did I, and for a whole hour we whispered Latin words and sentences and rules of syntax to one another, and I knew that it was all useless. At exactly ten minutes past three the haggard woman came out of the next room, bringing a strong smell of vinegar with her. She stroked the child's hair, looked at me and said, "Do you think she will manage it? She did all right on the last test. Tomorrow they are going to have another."

I buttoned up my coat, drew my wet beret out of the pocket, and said quietly, "She will make it all right." I laid my hand on the child's dull, fair hair and her mother said, "She must make it. She is all I have. My man was killed at Vinnitza." For an instant I saw the grimy railway station at Vinnitza, full of rusty tractors. Then I looked at the woman, and she suddenly took heart and said what she had been wanting to say for a long time, "May I ask you to wait for the money till . . ." I said yes before she had ended her sentence.

The child smiled at me. When I came out it had stopped raining. The sun was shining and large yellow leaves were floating down, one by one, on to the asphalt. I would have liked to go straight home to the Blocks with whom I have been living for a month, but I was overcome by the urge to do something, to make an effort, even though I knew it would be fruitless. I might have

10

asked Wagner for money or the Beisems' maid or the woman who smelled of vinegar. They would certainly have given me something. But now I went to the tramway station, got into a Number 11, and as I stood swaying in a crowd of wet passengers as far as Nackenheim, I became aware that the hot sausage I had swallowed at midday was disagreeing with me. I got out at Nackenheim and walked up between untended bushes till I got to the Bücklers' villa. His friend Dora let me in and took me into the living room. When I came into the room Bückler smiled rather stiffly, tore a strip from the edge of a newspaper to mark the page, and clapped his book to. Then he turned to greet me. He too has grown old. He has now been living for years with Dora and their relationship has become much more boring than marriage can ever be. They watch each other with a ruthlessness which has hardened their features, call each other "treasure" and "mouse" and are bound together by unbreakable chains.

When Dora came into the living room she, too, tore a strip from a newspaper and put it in her book. Then she poured me out a cup of tea. She and Bückler were sitting at a little table on which were sweets, cigarettes, and a teapot.

"Nice to see you again," said Bückler. "Cigarette?" I thanked him and took one. Dora sat with her face turned away from me and, whenever I turned to look at her, I noticed that her face had a stony expression which melted into a smile when she met my eyes. They both were silent and I said nothing. Then I stubbed out my

11

cigarette and broke the silence, saying, "I need money. Perhaps . . ."

Bückler interrupted me with a laugh and said, "Then you need what we have been needing for a long time. I would help you gladly, you know, but money . . ."

I looked at Dora and at once her stony expression softened into a smile. She had sharp lines round her mouth and it seemed to me that she was inhaling the smoke of her cigarette more deeply than usual.

"You must forgive me," said I, "but you know . . ."
"Yes, I know," said Bückler. "There is nothing to forgive. Anybody can get into difficulties."

"Well, I won't disturb you any longer," I said and stood up.

"You don't disturb us at all," he answered, and I knew from the tone of his voice, which suddenly came alive, that he meant what he said. Dora stood up too and pushed me back into my chair. I read in her eyes her fear that I should go away. I suddenly understood that they were really glad to see me. Dora handed me the cigarette case and poured me out another cup of tea, so I settled down and threw my beret on a chair. But we continued to sit in silence, interjecting a word here and there, and every time I looked at Dora her stiff expression dissolved into a smile which I felt was quite genuine. When at last I got up and picked up my beret, I realized that she and Bückler were afraid of being alone together, that they were afraid of their books, their cigarettes, and their tea, and dreaded the evening and the unending boredom they had prepared for themselves, because they were afraid of the boredom of marriage.

Half an hour later I was standing in another quarter of the town and ringing the doorbell of an old school friend. I had not been to see him for a year and when he pulled back the curtain which covered the tiny Judas window in his front door, I saw a disturbed look on his fat white face. Opening the door gave him time to put on another expression. As we went into the hall of his flat, the steam of a hot bath floated out of one of the doors and I heard the high voices of children. His wife called from inside, "Who is there?" I sat for half an hour with him in a sitting room furnished in shades of green which smelled of mothballs. We talked about various things as we smoked and when he began to tell old school stories his face lit up but boredom crept over me, and at last I blew a question into his face with the smoke of my cigarette. "Can you lend me some money?" He was not at all surprised but talked about the cost of the radio, the new kitchen cupboard, the new sofa, and his wife's new winter coat. Then he changed the subject and began to talk of school days again. As I listened to him, a ghostly feeling came over me. It seemed to me that he was talking of things that had happened two thousand years ago. I saw myself and the other boys in a dim and misty past fighting with the caretaker of the school, throwing sponges at the blackboards, smoking in the lavs, which reminded me of cabins in some remote and antique setting. Everything was frighteningly strange and far away, so I got up and said, "Forgive me for bothering you," and took my leave. His face grew surly again as we went through the hall and his wife's shrill voice again called out something from the bathroom which I could not understand, and he growled something back which sounded like, "Don't fuss," and the door closed behind me. I turned round and noticed that he had pulled back the curtain of the little window in the door and was watching me walk away.

I went slowly back into the town. It had begun to rain again but only a drizzle. Everything smelled damp and rotten and the gas lamps in the street were already lit. I went into a pub and had a schnapps. There I saw a man by a juke box. He kept putting coins into the slot to hear popular airs. I blew the smoke of my cigarette over the counter, gazed into the dismal face of the landlady, who looked like a damned soul, paid for my drink and made off.

The rain was running down into the street in muddy rivulets, yellow and brown, from the heaps of rubble formed by the Blitzed houses, and from the scaffoldings under which I walked chalky drops fell on the shoulders of my overcoat.

I went and sat down in the Church of the Dominicans and tried to pray. The building was dark but I could see small groups of men, women, and children standing by the confessional boxes. On the altar there were two lighted candles and near them the red light which is never put out. The confessional boxes were lit by tiny lamps. Though I was freezing, I stayed for nearly an hour in the church listening to the gentle murmur of voices confessing their sins and watching the people in line who made way whenever a penitent came out, walked to the central aisle, and covered his face with his hands. Once I saw the red glow of an electric fire, when one of the fathers opened the door of his box and looked round to see how many sinners were still waiting. I noticed that his face fell when he saw that there were still nearly a dozen. He went back into the box and I heard him turn out the electric fire and the gentle murmuring began again.

Then, in my mind's eye, I saw all the people with whom I had been since noon, beginning with the girl in the office who had given me a strip of sticking tape, the pink-faced woman in the sausage booth, my own face with mouth wide open to swallow bits of sausage meat and the faded beret on my head. I saw Wagner's face and the coarse but gentle face of the girl at Beisems' and the face of young Alphonse Beisem into which I had murmured the rules of fractions; the girl in the kitchen with its smell of vinegar; the railway station at Vinnitza full of rusty tractors where her father had met his death; her mother with her thin face and great yellowish eyes. I saw Bückler and the chap I had been at school with and the red-faced man who had stood by the automatic machine in the pub. I was getting too cold so I rose from my knees, took some holy water from the font by the door, and crossed myself. Then I went out into Böhnen Street and when I had got into Betzner's drinking shop and settled down in the corner by the automatic machine, I knew that during the whole afternoon, ever since I had taken the ten-mark note out of the envelope, I had been

15

thinking of nothing else but Betzner's little joint. I threw my cap on to a peg and called out, "A large rye, please." Then I unbuttoned my overcoat and looked for some coppers in my jacket pocket, put a penny in the slot of the pinball machine, pressed the knob, and released the nickel balls into the runway. With my right hand I took the glass of rye which Betzner had brought me and then I shot the first ball up into the field of play and heard the bells ring as it touched the obstacles. And when I searched deeper in my pocket I found the five-mark piece which a colleague had loaned me when he relieved me at the exchange. I had almost forgotten it.

I bent low over the table, watched the balls running and listened to their music, and I heard Betzner say softly to a man who was leaning against the counter, "That chap will stop there till he hasn't a penny left in his pocket."

KATE

I keep on counting the money Fred has sent me. There are all sorts of notes—dark green, light green, and blue. Notes stamped with the heads of peasant women bearing sheaves of corn, full-bosomed females symbolizing commerce or viticulture; a man wearing the mantle of some historic hero and holding a wheel and a hammer in his hands, who is probably meant to represent industry. Then comes a tiresome girl clasping the model of a bank building to her breast. At her feet are a scroll and an architect's instruments. In the middle of the green notes is an unattractive bitch with a balance in her right hand. She stares past me with lifeless eyes. The fringes of these

17

precious pieces of paper are decorated with ugly patterns. In the corner they bear the numbers showing their value. The coins are stamped with oak leaves, ears of corn, vine leaves, and crossed hammers, and on the reverse side they bear the fearful semblance of an eagle with outspread wings who is off on a flight of conquest.

The children watch me as I sort the notes and lay the coins in a heap. They represent the monthly wages of my husband who is the telephone operator in an ecclesiastical establishment. Three hundred and twenty marks and eighty-three pfennigs is what they pay him. I put aside one note for the rent, one for the electricity and gas, and one for the health insurance. I reckon up how much I owe the baker and make out that I have two hundred and forty marks left for myself. Fred put in a slip of paper to say that he had taken out ten marks which he will pay me back tomorrow. He will certainly spend them on drink.

The children watch me. Their faces are quiet and serious, but I have a surprise in store for them. Today they can play in the hall of the Frankes' flat. The Frankes are away over the week end at a conference of the Catholic Women's League. The Selbsteins, who live just below us, are away on a fortnight's holiday, and the Hopfs who have rented a room next door to us and only separated from our place by a thin wall—well, I haven't got to ask their permission. So the children can play in the hall and that is a privilege not to be despised.

"Did Father send that money?"

"Yes."

"Is he still ill?"

"Yes. Today you can play in the hall, but don't break anything and be careful of the wallpaper." It is a pleasure to me to see them happy and also to know that they are out of the way when I begin my Saturday chores.

The smell of jam and preserves still hangs about the hall although Mrs. Franke must long ago have finished making her three hundred pots. Mixed up with it is the smell of vinegar, which by itself is enough to turn Fred's stomach, and the smell of overcooked fruit and vegetables. The doors are locked and on the row of pegs there is only that old hat which Mr. Franke puts on when he goes into the cellar. The new wallpaper comes right up to our door, and the new painted dado comes up to the middle of the doorway leading to our dwelling. This consists of a single room in which we have made a sort of cubicle in plywood where our youngest sleeps and where we store odds and ends. The Frankes have four rooms all for themselves: kitchen, living room, bedroom, and a reception room in which Mrs. Franke receives her numerous visitors of both sexes. I don't know how many committees and boards she belongs to and I don't care what societies she is a member of: I only know that the Church Authorities have certified that she can't do without this room—this room which, if we had it, would not, perhaps, give us happiness, but would make it possible for us to live together.

At sixty Mrs. Franke is still a good-looking woman, but the famous brightness of her glance with which she fascinates everyone else just frightens me. Her hard, black eyes, her neat, well-dyed hair, her deep voice with a slight tremor, which, only when talking to me, can suddenly grow shrill, her well-fitting clothes, the fact that she goes to holy communion every morning and kisses the bishop's ring every month when he receives the leading ladies of the diocese—these things make her irresistible. We have learned this by experience, because we have tried for years to resist her and have now given up the struggle.

The children are playing in the hall. They are so accustomed to being quiet that they don't know how to play noisily, even when they are allowed to. I can hardly hear them. They have made a train out of cardboard boxes, tied together, which runs the whole length of the hall and is carefully towed backward and forward. They have put up stations where they load tin boxes on the train and little bits of wood for logs and I can be sure that they will be busy till suppertime. My little boy is still asleep.

Once more I count the notes, the precious, dirty notes, whose sweet, sickly smell gives me the creeps, and along with them I count the ten-mark note which Fred owes me. He will surely spend it on drink. Two months ago he left us. Now he sleeps with acquaintances or in some refuge, because he can no longer endure our cramped quarters and the presence of Mrs. Franke and those awful Hopfs who live next door. Some time back the Housing Board, which is putting up dwellings on the outskirts of the town, decided not to allot us one because Fred drinks and because the parish priest refused to recommend me. He is cross with me for not attending the functions of church societies. The chairman of the Housing Board is Mrs. Franke who, by her decision, has enriched her reputation for virtue and unselfishness for, if she had allotted a dwelling to us, our room, which she would like to have as a dining room, would have been free for her to take. So she decided against us and against her own interests.

Since then I have lived in fear—a fear which I cannot describe. The fact of being the object of such ill will inspires me with dread and I am afraid to partake of the Body of Christ, for Mrs. Franke's daily attendance at communion seems to make her more and more frightening. The brilliance of her glance grows harder and harder. I am afraid of going to mass too, though the gentle words of the liturgy provide me with one of my few remaining joys. It frightens me to see the parish priest at the altar: the same man whose voice I so often hear in Mrs. Franke's reception room. He has the voice of an inhibited sensualist who smokes good cigars and makes silly jokes to amuse the women of his committees and clubs. I often hear them through the wall laughing loudly, while I am warned to take care that the children make no noise which might disturb the meeting. I no longer bother to do this and let the children play as they will. But I am shocked to see that they are no longer able to play noisily. Often in the morning when the baby is asleep and the elder children are at school and I am out shopping, I steal for a few moments into a church at a time when there is no service and immerse myself in the infinite peace which streams forth from the presence of God.

Sometimes Mrs. Franke has an impulse to be kind, which frightens me more than her hatred. At Christmas she came and invited us to join a little party in her living room. As we walked through the hall I saw myself and our little family as in a looking glass, Clemens and Carla in front, then Fred, and myself in the rear with the baby on my arm. We looked as if we were walking into the depths of a mirror and I saw how poor we looked.

In their living room, which has not been altered for thirty years, I felt strange and out of place, as if I had strayed into another world. We don't belong to such pictures and such furniture. We have no right to sit at tables covered with damask linen. And the Christmas-tree decorations, which Mrs. Franke has managed to keep safe through the war, made my heart stand still with fear. The gleaming blue and golden balls, the hair and the doll-like faces of the glass angels, the Holy Child, made of soap, in a rosewood crib, earthenware figures of Mary and Joseph painted in bright colors, smirking under a plaster text proclaiming, "Peace on Earth"— this furniture on which a charwoman sweats for eight hours of the week at fifty pfennigs an hour, with the consolation of being a member of the Mothers' Union— all this ghastly tidiness fills me with fear. Mr. Franke sat in a corner smoking his pipe. His bony figure is beginning to fill out and I often hear his noisy tread as he comes up the stairs and his panting breath as he passes my room to go into his flat.

The children, too, are afraid of the fine furniture. They sit nervously on leather chairs, so shy and quiet that I could weep to see them.

There are plates for them with presents on them. Christmas stockings and the inevitable china savings box in the form of a pig which has been an indispensable feature of the Christmas festivities in the Franke family for the last thirty-five years.

Fred's face was dark and I saw that he was sorry we had accepted the Frankes' invitation. He stood leaning against the window seat, took a loose, crumpled cigarette out of his pocket, smoothed it out, and lit it.

Mrs. Franke filled up the glasses with wine and handed the children bright-colored porcelain mugs full of lemonade on which were painted pictures from the story of the Wolf and the Kids.

We drank. Fred emptied his glass at a single swallow, held it critically in his hand, and seemed to be savoring the taste of the wine. In such moments I can't refrain from admiring his realism. It is easy to read on his face a thought which it would be superfluous to express: "Two savings pigs, a glass of wine, and five minutes of sentimentality cannot deceive me into thinking that our room is big enough to contain us."

A cold leave-taking concluded this miserable party and I could foresee by the look in Mrs. Franke's eyes what she would say about it afterward and how she would add to our countless other faults the reproach of ingratitude and rudeness—two more stages upward in her progress toward a martyr's crown.

23

Mr. Franke talks very little, but when he knows that his wife is not there he often puts his head into our room and silently lays a slab of chocolate on the table by the door, and sometimes I find a bank note hidden in the paper we use for wrapping things up. Sometimes, too, I hear him talking in the hall with the children. He stops them as they go through, murmurs a few words, and the children tell me that he strokes their heads and calls them "my dears."

Mrs. Franke is quite different. She is talkative and lively but incapable of tenderness. She springs from an old trading family of our town, which from generation to generation has progressed through a series of different commodities. Starting with oil and flour, they advanced via fish and cloth to the wine trade. Then they took to politics, after which they declined to real-estate broker-age. I often think that nowadays the family are trading in the most precious of all commodities—in God.

Mrs. Franke very seldom shows signs of gentleness, but she does when she speaks of money. She pronounces the word "money" with a tenderness which frightens me, using just the intonation with which other persons pro-nounce the words "life," "love," "death," or "God"—a combination of tenderness and awe. The glint of her eyes grows softer and her features younger when she talks of money or her preserves—her two inviolable treasures. Often, when I am down in the cellar fetching coal or potatoes, I hear her counting her glass jam pots in the room next door. I hear her soft, murmuring voice count-ing the numbers as if she were gently chanting the cadences of some secret liturgy, and her voice makes me think of a nun at prayer. It frightens me and often, leaving my pail behind, I rush upstairs and press my children to my bosom, feeling that I have to protect them against something. The children look at me, half comprehending my anxiety—my son with adolescent eyes and my daughter with the soft brown eyes of a child—and hesitatingly they join in the prayers which I begin to intone, the sleepy drone of a litany or the words of "Our Father," which fall shyly from our lips.

But it is three o'clock and suddenly the noise that foretells the Sunday breaks out in the town. There is a clamor in the courtyard and I hear the voices which announce the Saturday afternoon holiday and my heart begins to freeze within me. I count my money once more, look at the deadly boring pictures on the bank notes, and at last decide to break into my money. The children are laughing in the hall and the little one is awake. I must get busy. As I raise my eyes from the table over which I was leaning when I began to reflect on our life, my glance falls on the cheap, unframed reproductions nailed on the walls of our room. I see the sweet female faces of Renoir and find them so strange that I can't imagine how only half an hour ago I was able to endure them. I take them down and quietly tear them in two and throw the pieces into the rubbish bin which I shall soon have to carry downstairs. My eyes survey our walls but nothing finds favor in my sight but the crucifix over the door and the picture of a man, which I can't identify, whose vague outlines and faint coloring have hitherto meant nothing to me. Now they have a meaning, though I don't clearly understand what it is.

FRED

It was just getting light as I left the railway station and the streets were still empty. My road ran obliquely past a block of houses whose walls had been repaired with ugly patches of rough cement. It was cold and in the station square a few taxi drivers stood shivering with their hands deep in their greatcoat pockets. Four or five pale faces under blue peaked caps turned toward me for a moment. They turned simultaneously, like puppets on a string, to look at me; then they snapped back into their former position with their eyes fixed on the station exit.

At this hour there weren't even any tarts on the street and when I slowly turned round I saw the long hand of the clock jerk up to nine. It was a quarter to six. I went down the street which passes the big blocks right-handed, and peered into the shop windows. Somewhere I was bound to find a café or a drink shop open or one of those stalls, which I certainly dislike but prefer to the station buffets with their lukewarm coffee and their flat, warmed-up bouillon, the taste of which reminds me of the barracks. I turned up the collar of my overcoat, pushed in the corners, and brushed off the mud from my trousers and the skirts of my coat.

The night before I had drunk more than usual and about one o'clock in the morning had gone into the station to Max, who often finds me a corner to sleep in. Max, whom I knew in the war, is employed in the left-luggage office, where there is a great radiator in the middle of the room surrounded by a wooden contraption with benches to sit on. Here everyone comes for a rest who is employed on the ground floor of the station: porters, cloakroom personnel, and elevator men. The wooden partition round the radiator is far enough away from it to allow me to creep inside. There is a broad recess below the level of the floor, which is dark and warm. When I lie there my heart is at peace. The drink which circulates in my veins, the deep, grumbling sound of trains arriving and leaving, the bumping of the baggage trucks and the humming of the elevators—sounds which in the dark sound to me still darker—all combine to put me to sleep. Sometimes I cry, as I lie down there, thinking of Kate and the children. I cry, knowing that the tears of a toper don't count, and I notice that I have no pangs of remorse and just simply feel sorrowful. I was already a drinker before the war, but people seem to have forgotten that and do not judge my low moral standards too harshly because they say, "He has been in the war."

I tidied myself up as carefully as I could before a mirror in the show window of a café. The mirror reproduced the reflection of my thin, delicate figure countless times as if in some fantastic skittle alley in which cream tarts and chocolate-crusted cakes swarmed around me. I saw myself there, a series of tiny little men in an avenue of pastry, each one confusedly smoothing his hair and hitching up his trousers.

I sauntered slowly on past cigar—and flower—shops, past fashion shops from the windows of which mannequins stared at me with their phony cheerfulness. Then I came to a street which branched to the right and seemed to consist almost entirely of wooden shanties. At the corner hung a great white streamer saying, "Druggists, we bid you welcome!"

The shanties were built into the ruins, crouching under the burned-out or tumbled façades of houses, in the midst of which tobacconists, drapers, and news vendors had their places of business. When at last I came to a snack bar, it was shut. I rattled the latch but got no answer. Then I turned round and at last saw a light. The light I saw was on the other side of the street. I went across and perceived that it came from inside a church. The gap, where the high Gothic window had been, had been scantily patched with undressed stone, and pinched in the middle of the hideous masonry was a small window of painted yellow glass which must have originally come from a bathroom. Through the four panes filtered a feeble, yellowish light. I stood and thought for a minute. It wasn't likely, but perhaps it might be warm inside. I walked up the ruinous steps to the church door which was undamaged. It was padded with leather. It was not warm inside the church. I took off my cap and slowly groped forward between the benches till I saw candles burning in a side chapel. I went on though I had made up my mind that it was colder in the church than outside. It was drafty—in fact the wind seemed to be blowing into the church from every quarter at once. The walls, in places, had not been properly patched with stone. The gaps had been filled in with slabs of hard board plastered together, between which the cement seemed to be oozing. In some places the slabs were disintegrating into detached layers and were becoming warped. Moisture dripped from the dirty bulges in the wall. I stood, hesitating by a pillar.

I could see a priest in a white surplice standing by a stone table on which were two lighted candles. His hands were raised in prayer, and though I could only see his back, I realized that he was freezing. For the moment it seemed to me that the priest was alone with his open missal, his upraised hands, and his freezing back. But then in the dim shadows below the flickering candles I recognized the blonde head of a girl, bowed forward in an attitude of devotion so deeply that I could see her long hair parted in two even strands on her back. By her was a boy who kept fidgeting and turning to right and left. From his profile, though the light was dim, I could recognize the open mouth, the swollen inflamed eyelids, the fat cheeks, and the curiously twisted lips of an idiot, and in the rare moments in which his eyes were shut, there was visible a surprising and exciting expression of contempt on his imbecile countenance.

The priest turned round—a pale-faced, raw-boned peasant. He looked in the direction of the pillar by which I stood, folded his hands, unclasped them, and murmured some words. Then he turned back quickly, bent over the stone table, and blessed the girl and the idiot boy with an almost comic solemnity. Strangely enough, though I was in the church, I did not feel myself included in the blessing. The priest turned again to the side altar, put on his skullcap, took the chalice in his hand, and blew out the right-hand candle. Then he walked slowly to the High Altar, bowed, and vanished into the black darkness. I saw him no more and only heard the creaking hinges of a door as he went out. Then I saw the girl for a moment with the light on her, when she got up from her knees and went up the steps to blow out the remaining candle. I noticed how gentle her face was and how simply devotional her bearing. She stood in the soft yellow light and I saw that she was really beautiful. She was slender and tall and her face was clear and shining and there was nothing foolish or undignified about her when she pursed her lips to blow out the candle. Then darkness covered her and the boy and I did not see her again till she came out into the gray twilight which filtered through the little window high up in the wall. Once again I was touched by the way she held her head and moved her neck as she walked calmly by me, giving me a short, searching look as she went out. She was beautiful and I followed her. At the entrance she turned and bowed once more to the altar, pushed the door open, and led the idiot out.

I walked after her. She went in the opposite direction to the railway station into an empty street flanked by heaps of rubble and shanties and I saw that she looked round from time to time. She was slight, almost thin, and seemed to be not more than eighteen or nineteen, and she towed the idiot child along with a firm and patient hand.

After a while more houses began to appear, with only occasional shanties interspersed among them. There were a lot of tramlines on the street converging in the same direction and I recognized the neighborhood as a part of the town which I seldom visit. I realized that the tramway depot must be here, for I heard the sound of shunting trams behind a reddish, roughly repaired wall and in the dim gray of morning I saw the dazzling light of welding torches and heard the hissing of oxygen containers.

I had been staring so long at the wall as I walked that I had not noticed that the girl had stopped. Now I had almost come up to her and found her standing before a shanty looking through a bunch of keys. The idiot was gazing upward at the flat, gray expanse of sky. The girl looked back at me again and I hesitated a moment as I passed her. Then I saw that the door she was opening was that of an eating house.

When she had unlocked the door I saw inside in the

gray morning light some chairs, a counter, and the dull metal surface of a coffee machine. A musty smell of old potato cakes floated out into the street, and I saw in the gloom in a blurred glass container two plates with rissoles heaped on them, some cold cutlets, and a large green bottle full of gherkins swimming in vinegar. The girl looked at me standing there. She was taking down the tin shutters. I looked her in the face and said, "Excuse me, are you opening now?"

"Yes," she said and took the last shutter down and carried it into the shop and I heard her put it in its place. Then she came back again and looked at me, so I asked her if I could come in. "Certainly," she said, "but it is still cold inside."

"Oh, that doesn't matter," I said and walked in. In the shop there was an unpleasant smell and I took a package of cigarettes out of my pocket and lit one. She had switched on the light and I was astonished to see how tidy everything was.

She said, "Extraordinary weather for September. By midday it will be hot again, but at present it's bitterly cold."

"Yes," I said, "extraordinary. The mornings certainly *are* cold."

"I'll light the fire," said she in a clear, prim voice. I noticed that she seemed embarrassed.

I nodded and took up my position by the wall at the end of the counter and looked round. The walls, which consisted of bare planks, were plastered with colored advertisements of cigarettes showing elegant gentlemen with graying hair offering their cigarette cases with an inviting smirk to ladies in low evening dresses, while in their other hands they held bottles of champagne; or mounted cowboys with an expression of devilish merriment on their faces, holding in one hand a lasso and in the other a cigarette, and trailing behind them large and absurdly blue clouds of tobacco smoke which streamed over the prairie as far as the horizon like a great silken banner.

The idiot boy was squatting by the stove and his teeth were chattering with cold. He had in his hand a wooden holder in which was stuck a stick of bright red candy. He was sucking steadily at this and two thin streams of syrup trickled from the corners of his mouth.

"Oh, Bernard," said the girl gently as she leaned down and wiped his mouth carefully with her handkerchief. Then she took the lid off the stove, crumpled up some newspapers and shoved them in, laid pieces of wood and coal briquettes on the top and held a lighted match to the rusty nozzle of the stove.

"Won't you sit down?" she said to me.

"Oh, thanks," I replied but remained standing. I was cold and wanted to stand near the stove and, in spite of the mild distaste which the presence of the idiot caused me as well as the bleak smell of cheap, cold food, the prospect of hot coffee and rolls and butter gave me pleasure. And as I stood I looked at the back of her white neck and noticed her cheap, darned stockings and the gentle movements of her head when she bent down to see how the fire was getting on.

At first there was only some smoke but after a bit I heard it begin to crackle. Tongues of flame spurted up from the coals and the smoke died down. Meantime the girl was crouching by my feet, poking at the nozzle of the stove with dirty fingers and often bending down to blow, and then I could see down the nape of her neck to her white, childish back.

Suddenly she got up, smiled at me, and went behind the counter, where she turned on the tap in the sink, washed her hands, and plugged in the electric coffee machine. I went to the stove, took off the lid with a hook, and saw that the wood was well alight and the briquettes beginning to burn. I heard the coffee machine humming and felt my appetite growing. It is always the same story. When I have had too much to drink the night before, I have a great desire for coffee and breakfast. But I still looked with aversion at the cold sausages in their crinkled skins and at the bowls filled with salad. The girl took a tin case full of empty bottles and carried it outside. Sitting alone with the idiot gave me a curious feeling of irritation. The child took no notice of me, but it annoyed me to see him sitting complacently there, sucking his beastly stick of candy.

I threw my cigarette away and started when the door opened and, instead of the girl, a priest came in. It was the same priest who had just said mass in the church. He had a round, pale peasant's face and was wearing a very tidy black hat. He said, "Good morning," and an expression of disappointment fell like a shadow across his face when he saw that there was nobody behind the counter.

I said, "Good morning," and thought, "Poor devil!" I had only just realized that the church in which I had been in the early morning was the parish church of the Seven Sorrows and I was perfectly familiar with the personal file of the parish priest. He had only moderate references; his sermons did not please his congregations, they were not sentimental enough; his voice was harsh. In the war he had performed no heroic action. He had been neither a hero nor a rebel. He had never received a decoration nor been crowned with the invisible halo of martyrdom. He had even blotted his record by returning to barracks after Lights Out had sounded. But that wasn't so bad as an extraordinary affair with a woman, which admittedly turned out to be platonic but which had revealed in him a degree of spiritual affection which made the authorities feel uncomfortable. The parish priest of Our Lady of the Seven Sorrows was one of the category of clergy whom the bishop classified as *gamma minus* or even as *delta plus*. Now his embarrassed disappointment was so obvious as to pain me too. I lit another cigarette, said, "Good morning," again and tried not to look at his commonplace face. Whenever I see clergymen with their black gowns and their look of innocent certainty—or is it innocent uncertainty?—I feel the same mixed feeling of rage and sympathy which I feel toward my own children.

The priest tapped nervously on the glass-plated counter with a two-mark piece. His face flushed from the neck upward when the door opened and the girl came in.

"Oh," he said hurriedly, "I only wanted some cigarettes." I watched him closely as he fished out a red

35

package of cigarettes from a heap with his short, white
fingers, taking care not to touch a pile of cutlets, which
he had to by-pass to get at the cigarettes. He threw the
coin on the counter and then, muttering, "Good day,"
in an almost inaudible voice, he left the shop.

The girl looked after him and put down the basket
which she had been carrying in the crook of her arm.
Meanwhile I felt the water come into my mouth at the
sight of the fresh, light-brown rolls. I swallowed, put my
cigarette out, and looked for a place to sit down. The
stove was now giving out a lot of heat, faintly tinged
with the smoky smell of the briquettes, and I felt slightly
sick as my hunger sent the bile from my stomach to the
back of my throat.

Outside, the curving tramlines screamed as streams
of dirty white trams left the depot and drove out on to
the street, trailing one behind the other, and finally
branched off from their shunting points on to their
several lines where the noise of their wheels gradually
faded in the distance. They made me think of white
strands fanning out from a ball of thread.

The water in the coffee machine began to bubble softly
and all the time the idiot-boy went on sucking his stick
of candy, which by now was almost finished.

"Will you have coffee?" asked the girl from the
counter.

"Yes, please," I said quickly and, as if touched by the
eager tone of my voice, she turned her pretty, peaceful
face to me and nodded, smiling as she pushed a cup and
saucer under the tap.

She carefully opened the canister containing ground coffee and took a spoon in her hand. I smelled the marvelous fragrance of the freshly ground coffee. She hesitated a moment and said, "How much? How much coffee do you want?"

I quickly took my money out of my pocket, smoothed out the notes, and counted the small change, fumbled again in my pocket, and then reckoned up what I had and said, "Oh, I must have three cups."

"Three?" she said, smiling, and added, "then I'll give you a coffeepot. It will be cheaper like that."

I watched her put four heaped teaspoonfuls of coffee on to a nickel slide which she pushed into the machine. Then she removed the cup from under the tap and replaced it by a coffeepot. She gently turned on the tap. The boiling coffee thumped and bubbled and a cloud of steam rose past her face. I could see the dark-brown liquid beginning to flow into the pot and my heart started racing with excitement.

I sometimes think about death and the moment of passing from this life to the next, and imagine to myself what there will be left for me to remember in this last minute. Will it be my wife's pale face, the candlelit ear of the priest in the confessional box, a few quiet masses in dim churches, the rosy, warm skin of my children, the schnapps coursing through my veins, a few breakfasts?— and at that moment as I looked at the girl handling the taps, I knew that she, too, would be in the picture. I unbuttoned my overcoat and threw my cap on to an empty chair.

"Can I have some rolls, too?" I asked. "Are they fresh?"

"Of course you can. How many do you want? They are quite fresh."

"Four," I said, "with butter."

"How much butter?"

"Oh, fifty grams."

She took the rolls out of a basket, put them on a plate, and began to slice butter off a half-pound package with a knife.

She divided the half-pound packet into four quarters, and I saw clearly that she gave me the largest of them. She stripped the paper from the butter and came to me with my breakfast on a tray.

She stood before me, holding the tray in one hand and trying to unfold a napkin to serve as a tablecloth with the other. I helped her to do this and for a moment was aware of the scent of her hands, which smelled good.

"There you are," she said.

"Many thanks."

I poured out my coffee, put sugar in the cup, stirred it, and drank. It was very hot and very good. Only my wife can make such good coffee, but I seldom drink coffee at home and I was wondering how long it was since I had tasted anything so good. I gulped down several mouthfuls without stopping and at once felt better. I called to the girl, "Your coffee is wonderful." She smiled at me and nodded and I suddenly realized how much I liked looking at her. Her presence filled me with well-being and ease.

She said, "No one has ever told me that my coffee is so good."

"But it is," I said.

Soon afterward I heard the clink of empty bottles in the container she had put outside, and the milkman came in with full bottles, which the girl checked with her white fingers—milk, cocoa, yogurt, and cream. It was now warm in the shop and the idiot-boy was still sitting there with the handle of the candy stick in his mouth, now and then uttering inarticulate sounds which all began with *tz* and seemed to contain a secret tune: *tzoo-tzoo, tza-tza, tzooo,* and there was a strange, wild rhythm in his gibberish. A grin of pleasure spread over his face when the girl turned to look at him.

Then some mechanics from the tramway workshops came in, took off their goggles, and, sitting down, drank milk through straws out of bottles. I noticed that the arms of the town were embroidered on their dungarees. Outside things were getting livelier; the long trains of trams had stopped and now the whitish cars rolled by separately in regular sequence.

I thought of Kate, my wife, with whom I was going to pass the night. But before I met her I would have to collect some money and get a room. It isn't easy to raise money and I wished I knew someone who would give it to me right away. But in towns like ours, with a population of three hundred thousand inhabitants, it is hard to find one who will do that. I knew a few people whom I did not mind asking, and made up my mind to go to them; and I thought I might call at some hotels on the way to see if I could get a room.

I had finished my coffee and it was close on seven. The shop was full of tobacco smoke; and a tired-looking, unshaved invalid came hobbling in with a smile on his face and sat down at a table by the stove, where he drank a cup of coffee and fed the idiot-boy with pieces of bread and cheese which he took from a package wrapped in a newspaper.

Meantime the girl stood behind the counter with a dishcloth in her hand, taking money, giving change, smiling and greeting the customers, handling the lever of the coffee machine, and drying the bottles with her dishcloth when she took them out of the hot water.

She seemed to do everything easily and without effort, although there was often a throng of impatient clients clustering at the counter. The steam of the coffee machine puffed past her face as she served hot milk, cold cocoa, hot cocoa, or fished gherkins with wooden tongs out of the dark-colored glass bottle. Then, suddenly, the shop was empty. Only a plump young fellow with a yellowish face was standing up by the counter holding a gherkin in one hand and a cold cutlet in the other. He finished them both quickly, lit a cigarette, and searched for his money which, it appeared, he kept loose in his pockets. I inferred from his brand-new suit, which was scarcely rumpled, and the fact that he was wearing a tie that outside they were keeping a holiday and that Sunday was beginning in the town, and it struck me that it would be very difficult to raise any money on a Sunday.

40

Finally the young fellow went too and I remained alone with the unshaven invalid, who perseveringly continued to push pieces of bread and cheese into the idiot-boy's mouth, while he quietly imitated the noises the boy made—*tzoo-tzoo, tza-tza, tzo-tzo*. But his mumblings lacked the wild, fascinating rhythm of the original. I watched the idiot meditatively as he slowly chewed mouthfuls of bread and cheese. The girl leaned against the wall and looked at the two of them. She was drinking milk out of a mug and eating an unbuttered roll from which she broke off pieces with her fingers. The atmosphere was calm and peaceful, but I noticed a sudden feeling of irritation rising in me.

I called out roughly, "I want to pay," and got up. I felt something like shame when the invalid looked at me with a cool, searching glance. The idiot, too, turned in my direction, but his watery, light-blue eyes wandered past me. In the silence the girl said, "Let him be, Father. I think Bernard has had enough."

She took the note from my hand and threw it into a cigar box under the counter. Then she slowly counted out my change on the glass sheet and when I had pushed over some coins as a tip, she took them, said, "Thank you," and took up her mug to drink some more milk. She still looked beautiful in broad daylight and I hesitated a moment before I went out. I would have liked to stay there for hours, sitting and waiting. I turned my back on the three and remained motionless; then I started into life, said, "Good day," and went quickly out.

In front of the door I found two young fellows in white

shirts engaged in unrolling a streamer and fixing it between two wooden posts. There were flowers scattered over the roadway and I waited a moment till the streamer was completely unrolled and then read in scarlet letters on a white background the text: "Hail to the Bishop, the Shepherd of our Souls."

I lit a cigarette and turned toward the city, where I had to raise some money and find a room for the night.

KATE

When I go to the tap to fill my pail, I see, without looking for it, my reflection in the mirror—a thin-faced woman, well acquainted with the bitterness of life. My hair is still thick and the few gray hairs on my temples, which give a silver sheen to my blondeness, are a faint sign of my grief for the loss of our two children to whom, my father confessor tells me, I ought to pray. They were the same age as Franz now is. They were beginning to sit up in bed and used to try to speak to me. They never played in flowery fields, but I often see them there, and the sorrow I feel at having lost them is mixed with a certain satisfaction when I think that they have been spared the bitterness of living. And yet I dream of two other imagined beings, growing up year by year and changing almost every month. They look just like what my little ones would have become. In the eyes of these two dream children, whom I see behind my likeness in the glass beckoning to me, is a wisdom which I recognize though I don't profit by it. For in the sadly smiling gaze of the twins, standing deep in the background of the mirror in a silvery twilight, I see an infinite patience—and I, I am not patient and will not give up the struggle as they seem to counsel me to do.

My pail fills slowly. The note of the running water sounds higher and thinner and as soon as I hear that the vessel which symbolizes my daily struggle is nearly full, my look comes back from the depths behind the mirror and rests for a second on my own face. My cheekbones are rather prominent, because I am getting thin. There is a yellow tinge on the natural pallor of my skin and I begin to wonder if I ought not to change the color of my lipstick for tonight and get myself a brighter red.

How many thousand times have I done what I now do again! I hear, without looking, that the pail is full: I turn the water off, grip the handle of the pail with both hands, stiffen the muscles of my arms, and with a heave swing the heavy bucket down to the ground. I listen at the door of the plywood cubicle we have made for Franz to be sure that the child is still sleeping.

Then my fight begins—my fight against dirt. I don't know what makes me hope that one day I shall win the battle. I hesitate for a few moments before I set to work, pass a comb through my hair without looking in the glass, clear away the breakfast things, and light half a cigarette which I had put in the cupboard between my prayer book and the coffee canister.

The people next door are awake. I hear the popping of the gas ring through the thin partition wall, the early-morning giggling of the neighbors and then the voices I loathe begin their chatter.

The husband seems to be still in bed. I can't understand his mumblings, and I only catch what the wife says when she turns in my direction.

". . . last Sunday eight real ones . . . fetch new rubbers . . . when will there be money . . ."

Now he seems to be reading out a cinema program for I suddenly hear her say, "Let's go to that." So it seems they will go to the pictures and to the pub and I begin to be rather sorry that I have made a date with Fred, for tonight it will be quiet, at least next door. However, Fred has already made his plans. He has probably booked a room and collected some money and we can't put off our rendezvous. And now my cigarette is finished.

Whenever I move the cupboard away from the wall pieces of plaster flake off and fall on the floor between the feet of the cupboard whence they spread all over the room in a tide of chalky fragments. Sometimes a regular slab falls from the wall, and as it disintegrates the dust flies all over the room; and the cloud now rising as I push the cupboard out warns me that today the battle will be a fierce one. Every object in the room is covered

45

with dust—a fine chalky powder—and I am obliged to go over everything a second time with the duster. The gritty dust grates under my feet and I hear the little boy coughing in his cubicle from inhaling the beastly stuff. I feel despair like some bodily pain. Fear gathers in my throat like a swelling which I try to swallow down. I choke violently as a mixture of dust, tears, and hopelessness slides down into my stomach. But it is only now that I accept the challenge and settle down to try conclusions with the dirt. With twitching face I sweep the plaster fragments into a heap after I have opened the window. Then I take the duster, wipe the dust carefully off everything, and finally plunge the cloth in water. As soon as I have struggled to clean a square yard of floor I am obliged to rinse out the cloth, which turns the clear water in the pail into a milky cloud. After the third square yard the water gets thick and sticky and when I empty the pail there remains at the bottom a horrid limey sediment which I must scratch out with my nails before I can rinse it away. And then I have to fill the pail once more.

Looking again into the mirror, past my own face, I see my two babies, Regina and Robert, the twins whom I bore to see them die. It was Fred who cut the navel cords, who boiled the instruments, who laid his hands on my forehead as I cried out in the throes of my labor . . . Fred, who heated the stove, rolled cigarettes for the two of us, and absented himself without leave from his regiment. I often think that I first began to love him when I realized how little he cared for rules and regulations. He took me in his arms and carried me into the cellar, and he was present when I first suckled my babies in the musty cool of the cellar by soft candlelight. Clemens sat on his stool and looked at a picture book, while the bombers roared over our house and passed onward.

But the threatening sound of the water in the pail, by now near to overflowing, calls me back to my battle with the dirt, and when, with the familiar movement, I swing the bucket down to the ground, I notice that the surfaces which I have just washed have dried and show a deadly film of white sediment which can't be extirpated. This vague whiteness kills my enthusiasm and wears down my strength, and the encouragement I get from the sight of the clear water in the pail is slight.

And so it goes on. Once more I lift the empty zinc bucket and place it under the slow-flowing stream of tap water and, as it fills, my eyes plunge deep into the milky, blurred distance in the back of the mirror. I see the bodies of my two lost children swollen with the bites of bugs and lice and it sickens me to think of this deadly host of vermin mobilized by a human war. As soon as the fighting starts, billions of lice and bugs, mosquitoes and fleas march into action, driven by a dumb instinct which tells them there is work to be done. Oh, I know and can never forget that death came to my twins through the lice and that we were supplied with some perfectly useless stuff from a factory run by a cousin of the Minister of Health, while the good, effective antidote was withheld from us. I know and can never forget it, for in the dim background of my glass I see my two little ones disfigured by vermin bites, feverish and crying with their little bodies swollen with useless injections. I turn off the tap again but this time without grasping the handle of the pail, because I remember that today is Sunday, and I want to pause for rest in my struggle against the plague of dirt which the war has set in motion.

I see, too, Fred's face growing inexorably older and drained of its virtue by a life which would have been and would be useless but for the love which it inspires in me. It is the face of a man who too soon lost interest in everything which other men have decided to take seriously. I see him very often in the glass, and more often than before since he ceased to live with us.

I have turned on the tap again and now I see myself in the depths of the glass and look with astonishment at my smiling face—the face of a stranger—as I listen to the rising note of the water running into the pail. I try in vain to recall my glance from the world behind the mirror and focus it on my own, my real face on which I know there is no smile.

In the far distance I see women, yellow-skinned women, washing their linen in slow-flowing streams and singing the while. I see black women digging in the crumbly earth. I hear the meaningless but fascinating drumming of idle men in the background. I see brown women treading the corn in stone troughs with their babies on their backs, while their men squat stupidly round a fire with their pipes in their mouths. And I see my white sisters in the tenement houses of London, New York, or Berlin, or in the dark alleys of the slums of Paris. I see their bitter faces listening in dread for a drunkard's shout. And far back in the mirror I see the hateful army advancing—the unknown, unsung hosts of vermin mobilizing to kill my children.

The pail has long been full and, though it is Sunday, I must go on fighting against the dirt.

For years I have been fighting to keep this one room clean. I let the pail fill up, shake the cloth out, and pour the dirty water down the sink. I calculate that my task will be ended when I have scratched out and rinsed away as much plaster sediment as the masons, merry fellows, put into the room sixty years ago.

I often look into the mirror; indeed, I do so whenever my eyes come back from the dreamland on the other side. They rest on the reflection of my own face, which has been gazing, lifeless and indifferent, at the invisible scenes beyond, and then I sometimes see it lit by a smile which must have fallen on it from the faces of my children and stuck there. Or else I see an expression of fierce resolve, of hatred and sternness, which does not shock me but rather makes me proud, for it is the sternness of a face that will never forget.

But today is Sunday and I am going to be with Fred again. The little one is sleeping, Clemens and Carla are at the Procession and from the courtyard I hear the sound of three church services, two concerts, a lecture, and the husky song of a Negro which pierces through all the other sounds and alone touches my heart.

". . . and He never said a mumbling word." Perhaps Fred will manage to beat up some money and we shall be able to go to a dance hall. I must buy some new lipstick. I can get it from the landlady downstairs and she'll trust me for it. It would be lovely if Fred could take me to dance. I keep hearing the soft, husky voice of the Negro coming through the drone of two watery sermons, and I feel my anger rising against the preachers and their twaddle, which floats up to me like a bad smell.

". . . dey nailed Him to the cross, nailed Him to the cross."

Yes, today is Sunday, and our room is full of the smell of roast meat and I am almost in tears, thinking how happy the children, who seldom get meat at all, will be.

". . . and He never said a mumbling word," sings the Negro. ". . . He never said a word."

FRED

I went back to the railway station, changed some money at a sausage shop, and determined to take things easy, it being Sunday. I was too tired and too depressed to visit all the people from whom I might be able to borrow money, so I decided to ring them up—at least those who had telephones. I often succeed on the telephone in giving my voice that casual tone which raises one's credit. It is a mysterious truth that real need, which can be heard in the tone of a voice or read in the expression of a face, has the effect of making people tighten their purse strings.

I found an empty telephone booth at the station and

51

went in. I wrote down the numbers of a few hotels and took out my pocketbook to look up the numbers of the people whom I could ask for money. I had a lot of pennies in my pocket and hesitated for some moments as I looked at the grimy old tariff notice hanging on the wall and the directions for use, covered with scribbles. At last I falteringly dropped two pennies into the slot. This never-ending hunt for money is gradually becoming a nightmare to me. The more trouble I take to get it, the more it gets on my nerves and I can't feel penitent for getting drunk. I selected the number of a man who, if anyone, would give me something, but I knew that his refusal would make everything worse, because I was much less willing to beg from the others on my list. I let my pennies lie in the machine and waited for a while. The sweat broke out on my forehead and my shirt stuck to the back of my neck, as I realized how much it meant to me whether I got money or not. Outside the booth I saw the shadow of a man who seemed to be waiting and I felt like pressing the other knob and getting my money back. Then the booth next to mine became free and the shadow vanished from my door. I still hesitated. Above me I could hear the rumble of trains moving in and out and the distant voice of the station loud-speaker. I wiped the sweat off my face and thought to myself that I would never in such a short time be able to raise enough money to take Kate out.

I would have liked to pray God that the man whom I was calling should give me the money at once but I was ashamed to do so. Suddenly I pulled myself together and took my left hand off the lever to prevent myself from stopping the call again. When I had dialed the last number there was a moment of silence and then I heard the connecting signal and saw Serge's library in which the telephone was now ringing. I saw the shelves full of books and the fine engravings on the walls and the window stained in bright colors with a picture of St. Cassius. Then I remembered the streamer with the text, "Hail to the Shepherd of our Souls," and recollected that it was Procession Day and I thought that Serge would probably not be at home. I sweated more violently and must have failed to hear Serge's voice the first time, for I heard him say impatiently, "Hullo, who's there?"

The tone of his voice took away all my courage and in a single second my mind was filled with questions. Would Serge, for instance, when I asked him to lend me money, be able to distinguish me, the borrower, from me, his employee? I said, "Bogner," as loud as I could, wiped the cold sweat off my forehead with my left hand, and waited for Serge to speak. I never shall forget how relieved I was when he answered in a much friendlier tone, "Oh, it's you. Why didn't you say who you were?"

"I was afraid," I said.

He was silent. I heard the trains rolling and the voice of the announcer in the station and through the door of my booth I saw the shadow of a woman's figure. I looked at my handkerchief. It was dirty and wet. Serge's voice struck me like a blow. He said, "How much do you need?"

Through the telephone I heard the splendid, deep

tones from the belfry of the Church of the Three Kings making a wild clangor in the receiver. I said quietly, "Fifty."

"How much?"

"Fifty," I repeated, flinching under the blow which he had unintentionally inflicted. But that is how it is. When anyone sees me or hears me, he knows that I want to get money out of him.

"What's the time?" he asked.

I opened the door of the booth, looked first into the sulky face of an oldish woman who stood there shaking her head in disapproval, looked over the streamer of the Druggists' Union at the clock in the station hall, and spoke into the receiver: "Half-past seven."

Serge did not answer at once. On the telephone I heard the deep-voiced bells from the church and outside, too, through the noise of the railway station, I heard the bells of the cathedral.

Then he said, "Come at ten."

I was afraid that he would hang up at once and said hastily, "Hullo, hullo."

"Yes, what is it?"

"Can I count on you?"

"You can," he said. "Good-by till then." I heard him hang up and I did likewise and opened the door of the booth.

I determined to keep my small change for telephoning and walked slowly into the town to look for a room, but it was very difficult to find one. Many strangers had flocked into the city to assist at the Procession, in addition to the usual influx which had not begun to abate, and conferences, which attracted intellectuals of various sorts to the town, were being held. Surgeons, philatelists, and the Catholic Welfare Organization had formed an agreeable habit of meeting once yearly under the shadow of the cathedral. They filled the hotels and drove up the prices, spending their traveling allowances freely. Now it was the turn of the druggists and a great many of these seem to have turned up for the occasion.

I saw them all over the place wearing in their button-holes little red flags, the badge of their union. The chilly morning air did not seem to have diminished their good humor. They talked shop cheerfully in the buses and trams as they hurried to committees and election meet-ings, and seemed to have decided to occupy all the middle-priced hotels for at least a week. There really was a tremendous number of druggists and many of them had brought their wives over the week end, which increased the difficulty of finding a double bedroom. The union was also holding an exhibition, and streamers in-vited the public to visit this representative collection of hygienic products. Here and there groups of religious people were to be seen in the inner town on the way to the marshaling point of the Procession. I noticed a parish priest surrounded by great gilded baroque lamps and red-clad choir boys and attended by a group of men and women in their Sunday best.

A toothpaste firm had hired an airship to drop tiny parchutes over the town, each carrying a tube of tooth-paste, while on the quay by the river was a huge cannon

which fired balloons into the air bearing the names of a
rival firm. Other surprises were announced, and it was
whispered that the playful advertisement of a great rubber firm had been sabotaged by the church.

At ten I went to see Serge. I hadn't found a room and
my head was buzzing with the refusals of pale-faced
landladies and the surly growls of porters who had not
been to bed. The airship had suddenly gone away and
the booming of the cannon on the quay was no longer
to be heard. When I recognized the sound of hymn tunes
coming from the southern part of the town I knew that
the Procession had got under way.

Serge's housekeeper showed me into the library and
before I had sat down, Serge came through the door
leading into his bedroom, and I saw at once that he had
money in his hand. I saw a green note and a blue one,
and in the hollow of his hand were coins. I looked on
the ground and waited till he came up to me.

Then I looked up and the expression on my face made
him say, "Good heavens, it isn't as bad as all that."

I did not contradict him.

"Come here," he said. I held out my hands and he put
the two notes in my right hand and heaped the nickels
on top of them saying, "Thirty-five. I really cannot
manage more."

"Oh, thank you," I said.

I looked at him and tried to smile but could only
gulp helplessly. It was probably a painful moment for
him too. His tidy, well-brushed cassock, his clean, well-
kept hands, his perfectly shaven cheeks—everything

about him brought home to me the shabbiness of our dwelling and the poverty which for ten long years we have been breathing like a white dust. Yes, I feel poverty like a dust untastable, imperceptible, invisible, and indefinable, but real—a dust which haunts my lungs, my heart, and my brain—a dust which controls the circulation of my blood and which now made me lose my breath and cough.

I said wearily, "Good-by, then, and many thanks."

"My regards to your wife."

"Thank you," I said. We shook hands and I went to the door. I turned round before I left the room, and saw him standing, looking at me with his hand raised in blessing. I turned the door handle and slunk out with hanging, hopeless arms and a bright red flush on my face. Outside it was cold and I turned up the collar of my coat. Then I walked slowly into the town, where I heard the distant chanting of hymns and the long-drawn sound of trombones. Women's voices came through and then were drowned by the entry of a male choir. Gusts of wind brought the singing nearer, and the sound of much-rehearsed music mingled with the dust which blew about the heaps of rubble. Each time the dust blew up into my face, I was touched by the pathos of the singing. But suddenly the music stopped and twenty yards farther on I found myself in the street through which the Procession was passing. There were not many people on the sidewalks and I stopped and watched.

Wearing the blood-red garb we associate with martyrs, the bishop strode alone between the groups of communi-

57

cants and the Choral Society. The singers, flushed and
foolish-looking, gazed at him with perplexed faces as
if they still were listening to the soft music which they
had just ceased to make. The bishop was very tall and
thin and his thick white hair welled out from beneath
his tightly fitting red skullcap. His bearing was erect
and I noticed that, though he marched with folded hands
and looked straight in front of him, he was not praying.
The golden cross on his breast swung gently from side
to side to the rhythm of his steps. He had a long and
princely stride, and at each pace he raised his feet shod
in Moroccan leather rather high so that one could not
help thinking of a modest variety of the goose step. He
had been an officer. His ascetic face was photogenic and
would look well on the cover of an illustrated religious
magazine.

The cathedral clergy followed him at a short interval.
Only two of them had the good fortune to look ascetic.
The others were all fat and their faces either very pale
or very red, and they all looked indignant though one
could only guess why.

The gorgeous embroidered canopy was carried by
four men wearing dinner-jacket suits and under it walked
the Suffragan bishop with the monstrance.

I could just see the Host and I knelt down and crossed
myself. For a moment I had the feeling of being a hypo-
crite until it came to my mind that God was not to
blame for the inadequacies of his servants and that it
was no hypocrisy to kneel before Him. Almost everyone
on the sidewalks knelt down; only a young man wearing

a green corduroy jacket and a beret remained standing with his cap on his head and his hands in his pockets. It was some satisfaction to see that at least he wasn't smoking. When an old man with white hair came up to him from behind and whispered something to him, he shrugged his shoulders and took off his beret which he held flat against his stomach. But he did not kneel.

I suddenly felt very sad as I watched the Procession of the Host moving on down the broad street and saw the people kneeling, getting up again, and brushing the dust off their knees in succeeding waves of movement.

Behind the group which surrounded the Host came a troop of some twenty men in evening clothes. Their dinner suits were all neat and well fitting except those of two men who I saw at once were workmen. They must have hated walking with the others whose clothes fitted them because they were their own. Theirs had obviously been borrowed. It is well known that the bishop has a highly developed social conscience and, no doubt, he insisted that workmen should be among the bearers of the canopy.

A company of monks came by. I liked the look of them. Their dark clothes covered yellowish-white habits and their neat tonsures on their bowed heads made a fine picture. And they did not have to fold their hands, but could hide them in their long, wide sleeves. The monks moved onward with bowed heads in perfect silence, not too fast or too slow, at a steady devotional tempo. Their broad collars and long robes and the blending of black and white gave them an aspect at once youthful and intelligent, and the sight of them could have made me wish to enter a monastic order. However, I know some of them personally and know that when they wear the uniform of secular priests they don't look any better than the others.

Some of the university people—there were about a hundred of them—had very intelligent faces; a few of them looked painfully clever. For the most part they were in evening dress but some of them wore ordinary dark lounge suits.

Then came the vicars of the different parishes in the town marching between lines of great baroque hand lamps, and I perceived how difficult it is to cut a good figure in the baroque trappings of an ordinary priest. Some of them were very fat and healthy-looking. I thought that the majority of the spectators on the pavement looked ill, run-down, and somehow at a loss.

The students all wore bright-colored caps and sashes and some of those in the middle of the group bore bright heavy silk banners. There were seven or eight groups of students each carrying three banners, one behind the other. All in all, this was the brightest group I have ever seen in any procession. The faces of the students were very serious and they all looked fixedly, unblinkingly, on some distant, fascinating goal. None of them seemed aware of anything comic in their attitude. One of the students, a chap wearing a red, blue, and green cap, had the sweat pouring down his face in streams, though the weather wasn't hot. He made no movement to wipe off the sweat and, to tell the truth, did not appear ridiculous but merely very unhappy. I thought to myself that he would probably be brought before a Court of Honor and kicked out of his fraternity for unauthorized sweating in a religious procession, and I felt that it was all up with his prospects of a career. And, indeed, he gave the impression of being a man without hope of success, while his dry-skinned companions looked as if they would certainly give him no chance of succeeding.

Next a group of school children came by. They were singing out of time: those in front were singing much too fast and those behind much too slow, so that three seconds after the leaders had finished one could hear the words they had sung coming from the rear guard. It sounded as if they were singing in canon. A few young teachers in new dress clothes and two young priests in lace surplices ran to and fro and tried to get some proper tempo into the singing by beating time with their arms, but their efforts to convey the spirit of correct rhythm from the front to the rear of their flock were quite unavailing.

I suddenly became giddy and could no longer see the people in the Procession and those who were watching it. The section in my field of vision suddenly shrank as though it had been screwed together and there in the midst of the flickering gray mass I could see nothing but my two children, Clemens and Carla. The boy was very pale. He looked rather tall in his blue suit with the green sprig of a first communicant in his buttonhole and a taper in his hand. His lovable, serious face was pale and collected. His sister, who takes after me with her round face, dark hair, and slender figure, was smiling a little. I seemed to be very far away from them but I saw them clearly. It was like a glimpse into an unfamiliar region of my life, like the sight of a strange burden that I have to bear. And when I looked at these children of mine, slowly and solemnly marching across my line of sight, I realized, as I had always known but never realized before, how poor we are.

I became entangled in the mass of people streaming toward the cathedral to assist at the service that would close the festival. For a time I tried in vain to break out of the throng to one side or the other, but I felt too tired to force my way through the mass. I let myself be carried by the stream, pushing slowly outward. I found the crowd repulsive and began to hate them.

As long as I can remember I have been against corporal punishment. I have always been upset at seeing anyone beaten in my presence and, whenever I could, I have tried to stop it, even in the case of prisoners. My unwillingness to watch prisoners being beaten made me an object of mockery and caused me much trouble and even danger, but I have never been able to conquer my aversion, even if I had wished to. I could not bear to see a man beaten or mishandled, but when I interfered, it was not from pity or love, but simply because the thing was unbearable to me.

But during the last few months I have often felt tempted to strike someone in the face, and, in fact, I have sometimes beaten my children because the noise they made irritated me when I came home tired from work. I beat them hard, very hard, well knowing that I was doing wrong, and it shocked me to feel that I was losing control over myself.

Suddenly, without warning, I am possessed by a wild desire to strike someone in the face. I wanted to slog the thin woman, moving along in the crowd so near to me that I could smell her sour, stale odor. Her face was one grimace of hatred, and she kept shouting at her husband who was in front of us—a quiet-looking, narrow-shoul-dered man in a green felt hat. "Hurry up," she cried. "Can't you go faster than that? We are going to miss the mass."

At last I succeeded in getting out of the stream on the right-hand side and stood in front of the window of a shoe shop and let the crowd pass by. I felt for the money in my pocket and counted the notes and the coins and made sure that nothing was missing. I wanted a cup of coffee but had to be careful with my money.

Suddenly the street was empty of people and all that remained was the dirt, the trampled flowers, the fine cement dust from the ruins, and the crooked streamers which had been hung up between disused tramway stand-ards. Printed in black on a white cloth background were the words, "Praise the Lord with joy. May Our Lady bless our Union." Many of the streamers had pictures of lambs, chalices, hearts, and anchors.

I lit a cigarette and strolled slowly toward the northern quarter of the town. In the distance I could still hear the singing from the Procession, but after a few minutes it ceased and I knew that it had reached the cathedral. People were coming out of a morning cinema show, and I ran into a group of young intellectuals who had already started to discuss the film they had just seen. They wore duffel coats and berets, and the boys had all gathered round a very pretty girl wearing a vivid green pullover and a pair of drill jeans.

"Awfully commonplace . . ."

"Yes, but the technique . . ."

"Imitation Kafka . . ."

I couldn't forget the children. I seemed to be able to see them with my eyes shut—the boy already thirteen and the girl eleven. Pale creatures destined for the treadmill. The two elder ones enjoyed singing but I had forbidden them to sing when I was at home. Their gaiety and the noise they made irritated me, and I had slapped their faces and beaten them on their behinds—I who couldn't stand the sight of corporal punishment—because I wanted to have quiet in the evening when I came back from work.

I could hear singing from the cathedral—religious music floating in waves down the wind. Then I turned to the left and went past the station. There I saw a group of men in white taking down the religious texts from the poles and fastening on new streamers bearing the words "German Druggists' Union," "Visit the Exhibition," "Many Free Samples," "What Are You Without Your Druggist?"

Slowly, without realizing where I was going, I wandered along to the Church of the Seven Sorrows and

64

went on without looking up, to the eating house in which I had breakfasted. It was almost as though in the morning I had counted my steps, and now a mysterious rhythm controlling my muscles had driven me back to the same place, forced me to stop, and made me look up. I did look up and saw through an opening in the curtains on the right the plate with a pile of cutlets and the big, highly colored advertisements of cigarettes. I opened the door and went in. Everything was quiet and I saw at once that she was not there; neither was the idiot-boy. A tramway man was sitting in the corner shoveling soup down his throat and at a table nearby were sitting a couple with unwrapped packages of buttered rolls and cups of coffee in front of them. The invalid now got up from behind the counter. He saw me and seemed to recognize me. His mouth twitched slightly. The couple and the tramway man also stared at me. The invalid said, "What can I do for you?"

"Five cigarettes," I answered, "the red brand." I took a coin out of my pocket and put it on the glass top of the counter. Then I put the cigarettes in my pocket, said, "Thanks," and waited.

I looked slowly round the room. They all continued to stare at me. The tramway man had his spoon poised in mid-air between his plate and his mouth, and I saw the yellow soup dripping from it. The couple stopped munching their rolls—the man's mouth was open and the woman's shut. Then I looked at the invalid. He smiled and through the dark, rough, unshaven skin of his face I recognized his daughter.

In the silence he asked me, "Are you looking for someone?"

I shook my head, turned toward the door, stood still a moment, and felt the eyes of the others in my back, and then I went out.

The street was still empty. A drunken man staggered out of the dark subway behind the station. He zigzagged clumsily almost on top of me and when he was within a foot of me I recognized the druggists' flaglet in his buttonhole. He stopped in front of me, caught hold of one of my coat buttons, and blew a reek of sour beer into my face as he hiccuped, "And what are you without your druggist?"

"Nothing," I said quietly, "without my druggist I am nothing."

"There, you see," he said contemptuously.

Then he released my coat button and staggered on and I went slowly into the dark subway.

Behind the station everything was quiet. Over the whole quarter hung a bittersweet scent of ground cocoa beans, mixed with the smell of caramels. A huge chocolate factory with its buildings and overhead gangways covers an area traversed by three streets and gives the quarter a gloomy appearance which contrasts with its appetizing products. Here is where the poor live. The few hotels one finds in these parts are cheap and the Tourist Union abstains from sending strangers to them for fear they should be shocked by the prevailing poverty. The narrow streets were filled with the smell of cooking—the odor of steamed cabbage and the stronger savor of roasting meat. Children sucking candy sticks stood around and through the open windows I saw some men in shirt sleeves playing cards. On the burned wall of a Blitzed house I saw a large, dirty signboard on which was painted a black hand and under it the words, "Holland Court: Rooms to Let: Good Plain Cooking: Dancing Sundays." I followed the directions to which the black hand pointed and found another black hand at the corner of the street with the inscription: "Holl. Ct. Directly Opposite." When I looked up at the red brick house in front of me, darkly coated by the smoke of the chocolate factory, I knew that the druggists had not penetrated as far as this.

KATE

I never cease to wonder at the way Fred's voice excites
me when I hear it on the telephone. His voice is hoarse,
it sounds tired, and it has a note of official indifference
which makes him seem strange to me and thereby excites
me the more. I have heard that tone from Odessa, from
Sebastopol, from countless public houses where he has
been drinking, and how often has my heart fluttered
when I have heard him press the knob and make the
contact! I know so well the quiet buzzing in the office
before he speaks, his cough, the tenderness of his voice
on the phone. And now he has called me again. When
I came down the main staircase, the landlady was sitting

in her corner on the sofa in the midst of her shabby furniture. The writing table was piled high with cardboard soap boxes, cases full of contraceptives, and wooden boxes in which she keeps her most costly cosmetics. The room was full of the smell of singed hair that had been treated from morning to night on the Saturday. Mrs. Baluhn herself was slovenly and her hair was disheveled. She had a novel from the lending library open in front of her, but she stopped reading it, preferring to keep her eyes on me as I put the receiver to my ear. Then she reached into the corner behind the sofa and, still looking at me with her weary eyes, fished out a bottle of schnapps and poured herself out a glassful.

"Hello, Fred," I said.

"Kate," he answered, "I have a room and I've got some money."

"Ah, that's good."

"When will you come?"

"At five. I've still got to bake some cakes for the children. Are we going to dance?"

"Gladly, if you want to. There is dancing here in the hotel."

"Where are you?"

"In Holland Court—a hotel."

"Where's that?"

"North of the station. Go along Station Road until you see a black hand painted as a signpost at the corner. The stretched-out finger points in the direction you have to go. How are the children?"

"All right."

"I've bought some chocolates for them and we'll get some balloons and I mean to stand them an ice. I'll give you the money to buy the things and I want you to tell them I'm sorry I . . . I beat them. It was wrong of me."

"I can't say that to them, Fred."

"Why not?"

"Because it will make them cry."

"Let them cry, if they must, but they have got to know that I am sorry. It is very important to me. Think it over, please."

I did not know what to say to him. I looked at the landlady who, with a knowing gesture, filled up her glass of schnapps again and raised it to her lips. She let the liquor roll round her tongue, and I perceived a slight twitch of revulsion on her face as the stuff flowed down her throat.

"Kate," said Fred.

"Yes?"

"Say everything to the children, please, and don't forget. Tell them about the chocolates and the balloons and the ice. Promise me you will."

"I can't," I said. "Today they are so happy because they are allowed to walk in the Procession. I am not going to remind them of the beatings. I'll tell them what you say later, sometime when we are speaking of you."

"Do you speak of me?"

"Yes. They ask me where you are and I tell them you are ill."

"Am I ill?"

"Yes, you are ill."

He was silent and I heard him breathing in the receiver. The landlady winked at me and nodded her head emphatically.

"Perhaps you are right and I really am sick. Anyhow, good-by till five. Don't forget. The sign with the black hand at the corner of Station Road. I have enough money and we'll go dancing. So long, dearest."

"So long."

I slowly replaced the receiver and saw the landlady put a second glass on the table.

"Come on, young woman," she said in a soft voice, "and drink a glass with me."

In the past I have often indignantly run downstairs to complain about the state of our room, but our landlady has always got the better of me by the insuperable force of passive resistance. She would pour me out a glass of schnapps and win me over with her weary, wise eyes. She managed to make it clear to me that it would cost her more to renovate our room than she would get from three years' rent. It was from her that I learned to drink schnapps. At first the brandy used to burn me and I asked for a liqueur instead. "Liqueur?" she said, "Who drinks liqueurs?" Since then I have persuaded myself that she is right. Her cognac is really good.

"Now come, my girl, you must have a drink," she said, and I sat down opposite her. She looked at me with the fixed stare of a drinker and my eyes looked past her face at a pile of brightly colored cartons bearing the label, "Griss Rubber Goods. Fine quality. Only genuine with the Stork trade-mark." "Here's luck," she said, and I raised my glass and said, "Good luck," and let the heart-warming, glowing liquor run down my throat. I understood at that moment why men take to drink: I understood Fred and all the other topers of the world.

"Ah, my child," and she filled my glass with a speed which astonished me. "You mustn't come any more to complain. There is no cure for poverty. Send me the children here this afternoon. You are going out, aren't you?"

"Yes," I said, "I'm going out, but I have engaged a young man to stay with the children."

"To stay the night?"

"Yes, to stay the night."

A faintly lascivious expression seemed to puff her face out for a second, like a yellow sponge; then her features sank back to normal.

"Oh, well," she said, "then you must let me give you some empty boxes for them to play with."

I thanked her. Her husband had been a broker. He had left her three houses, the hairdressing salon, and a collection of boxes.

"Let's have another drink."

"Not for me, thank you," I said.

I have noticed that her trembling hands become steady as soon as they touch the bottle, and her movements when she is handling it have a gentleness which startles me. She filled up my glass again as well as her own.

"Oh, please," I said, and she said, "Oh, very well, then, I'll drink it." Then suddenly she screwed up her eyes and looked intently at me saying, "Are you expecting, dear child?"

I shrank from the question. I have several times lately thought I was, but I'm still not sure. I shook my head.

"Poor child," she said, "that will be hard for you. Another little one to add to your burdens."

"I don't know," I said uncertainly.

"You must change the color of your lipstick, my dear," she said, looking at me again with a searching glance. Then she stood up and maneuvered her heavy body in its bright-colored smock between the armchair, the sofa, and the writing table on her way to the salon next door.

"Come," she said, and I followed her into the salon. The smell of hot air and perfumes from the sprinklers was as thick as a cloud and in the darkness of the curtained room I saw the permanent-wave machines, the helmets for drying, and a pale shimmer of nickel.

"Oh, do come along," she said, and fumbled in a drawer in which curling papers, loose lipsticks, and colored compacts were lying around in disorder. Then she picked up a lipstick, handed it to me, and said, "Try this one." I unscrewed the top of the brass sheath and looked at the dark red stick standing up like a frozen worm.

"As dark as that, do you think?" I asked.

"Yes, that's right. Put some on."

These looking glasses down here are quite different from mine upstairs. One can't look into the back of them and they keep one's face right in the foreground, making it look flat and very near and prettier than it is. I opened my lips, leaned forward, and colored them carefully with the dark red paint. My eyes aren't accustomed to these mirrors and I get the impression that there is another pair of eyes looking over my shoulder into my face in the glass. My head was swimming and I shuddered when I felt the hand of the landlady on my shoulder and saw her boozy face and tousled hair behind me in the mirror.

"Make yourself pretty, poppet," she said softly. "Make yourself pretty for love but don't go on creating children. That's the right color for you, child, isn't it?" I stepped back from the mirror, screwed the lipstick back in its case, and said, "Yes, that's the color, but I haven't any money to pay for it."

"Oh, don't fuss. You can pay for it later."

"Yes, later," I repeated. I went up and looked once more into the glass, skidded about inside it, as on an ice rink, held my hand before my eyes, and at last stepped back away from it.

Mrs. Baluhn heaped empty cartons on my outstretched arm, put the lipstick in the pocket of my apron, and opened the door for me.

"Many thanks," I said. "Good-by."

"Good-by," she echoed.

I don't understand how Fred gets in such a rage about the noise the children make. I find them so quiet. When I am standing before the fire or by the table, they are often so silent that I turn in a sudden excess of fear to make sure that they are really in the room. I find them building houses with empty boxes and whispering to one another, and when I turn to look for them, the fear in my eyes makes them run up to me and ask, "What is it, Mummy? What's the matter?"

Then I say, "No, it's nothing," and turn and go on rolling out the dough. I am afraid to leave them alone. Formerly I used to be away with Fred only in the afternoons. Since he left home I have only once spent a whole night with him. The little boy is asleep and, if I can manage it, I'll be gone before he wakes up.

Next door that awful groaning has stopped and the cooing and panting which accompany the love-making of our neighbors, the Hopfs. Now they have gone to sleep before going to the cinema. I am coming to the conclusion that we must buy a radio to drown the noises next door. The artificially loud conversation which I start as soon as the Hopfs get busy with their horrid duet—and I must admit that the noises they make inspire me with horror and not with contempt—well, it dries up so quickly and I ask myself whether the children are not beginning to understand what is happening. In any case, they hear the sounds and the expression on their faces is like that of trembling animals who smell the scent of death. When I can, I send them out into the street to play, but these early Sunday afternoons are so depressing that they even get the children down. I feel my face going red as fire as soon as these rare and painful silences set in in the next room, and I try to sing when the noises on the other side of the wall announce that our neighbors are struggling together. We hear the irregular bumping of the bedstead and the answering cries of the couple, which remind me of the way trapeze artists call to one another, high up at the top of the circus when they swing out toward one another and change trapezes in the air.

But my voice is cracked and unsteady, and when I try to sing the tunes that I have in my head, I can't get them. For long minutes during these deadly Sunday afternoons I hear my neighbors panting with exhaustion and then I hear them lighting cigarettes and I know that the silence which now reigns in their room is filled with hatred. I slap the dough on the table and roll it out as noisily as I can backward and forward, slap it down again and think of the millions of poor people who live and have lived and have never had a quiet place of their own to make love in. So I go on rolling out the dough, molding it into shape and stuffing currants into the cake.

FRED

The room was dark: it lay at the end of a long corridor.
Looking out of the window I saw a dingy brick wall
which must once have been red. It was decorated with
a pattern of yellow tiles which meandered along in a
serpentine design. Beyond the wall which ran obliquely
across my field of vision I could see the two platforms
in the railway station. Both of them were almost empty. I
could make out a woman sitting on a bench with a child
and the girl from the lemonade stall standing in front
of the door and rolling her white apron up and down
restlessly. Behind the station was the cathedral dressed
with flags for the feast, and it somehow depressed me

to see behind the empty station crowds of people clustering round the open-air altar. I found the silence of the
crowd in the cathedral depressing too. Then I saw the
bishop in his red robe standing near the altar and, as I
caught sight of him, I heard his voice ringing full and
clear from the loud-speaker across the empty railway
station.

I have often heard the bishop preach but his sermons
have always bored me—and I know nothing worse than
boredom—but now, as I heard his voice on the loud-
speaker, I suddenly found the adjective for which I had
long been searching. I knew that there was a simple
epithet to describe the Right Reverend which had often
been on the tip of my tongue and always had eluded me.
The bishop loves to put into his voice that touch of dialect
that makes a voice popular; but the bishop is not popular. The vocabulary of his sermons seems to have been
gathered from some catalogue of theological catchwords,
which during the past forty years have imperceptibly
but progressively lost their power to convince. Catchwords which had faded into empty phrases and half-
truths—his discourses bristled with them. Truth is not
boring but the bishop has the gift of making it seem so.

"Let us take God into our daily lives . . ."

For a few minutes I listened to his voice wafted across
the empty station to me and looked at the man in red
standing behind the loud-speaker and putting just a little
too much dialect into his pronunciation. Then the word
I had so long been looking for came to me. I suppose it
was too simple to have occurred to me before. The bishop
was stupid.

I looked back over the railway station where the lemonade girl was still rolling and unrolling her apron, while the woman on the bench was giving her child some milk out of a bottle. My glance wandered over the yellowish pattern of the tiles, snaking across the brick wall, and came back across the dirty window ledge to the room in which I stood. I shut the window, lay down on the bed, and lit a cigarette.

I could no longer hear the bishop and inside the house all was quiet. The walls of my room were papered in red with a green pattern in the form of a heart. But the pattern had become so faint that it looked like the scribbling of a pale pencil which astonishes one by its regularity. The lamp was ugly, like all such lamps. It was just an egg-shaped glass container, veined in blue, and it probably held a fifteen-candle-power bulb. I could see that the narrow cupboard, stained dark brown, was never used and, indeed, was not meant to be used. The sort of people who hire this room don't unpack their luggage, if they have any. They have no skirts to hang up or shirts to lay in layers, and the two coat hangers I saw in the open cupboard were so flimsy that the mere weight of my jacket would have been enough to break them. In this place one hangs one's jacket over the back of a chair and throws one's trousers over it without bothering to fold them, if, indeed, one takes them off at all. Meanwhile the other chair is occupied by the clothes of the pale or, possibly, rosy-cheeked female lying on the bed. The wardrobe is superfluous. It has a purely official existence like the coat hangers which have never been used. The washstand was a simple kitchen table fitted with a wash basin which could be lowered out of sight, but now it was visible. It was made of enameled zinc and was slightly chipped. There was an earthenware saucer for soap, an advertisement sample from a sponge factory. The tooth glass seems to have been broken and never replaced: at any rate there wasn't one. It appeared that the landlord had thought it his duty to do something in the way of mural decoration, and what could there be more appropriate than an oleograph of the "Mona Lisa" which looked as if it had been torn out of some popular art magazine. The beds were still new and had a sharp smell of freshly carpentered wood. They were low and dark. For the moment I was not so interested in bed linen as I was lying fully dressed waiting for my wife who would probably bring sheets with her. The blankets were of green wool and were somewhat threadbare. Woven into them was a design of bears playing ball, but the faces of the bears were worn out and no longer recognizable and the design looked more like a picture of bull-necked atheletes blowing bubbles at one another. The church clocks struck twelve.

I got up and brought the soap saucer to my bedside to serve as an ashtray, and began to smoke again. As I lay there thinking, it seemed to me dreadful that I had not been able to talk to anyone or explain my real situation to any other human being. I had borrowed money without saying why I wanted it. I wanted it because I needed a room so as to be able to sleep with my wife. For the last two months, though we both lived in the same town, we had enjoyed the intimacy of married life only in hotel rooms. When the weather was really warm we had been able to make love in one of the parks or in the passages of Blitzed houses in the heart of the town where there was no danger of being surprised. Our own home is too small. Enough said. And, besides, the partition wall between us and our neighbors is too thin. To get a bigger dwelling one needs money and one needs what they call energy, and we have neither money nor energy. Even Kate has no energy left.

The last time we met we were in a park together in a suburb outside the town. It was evening and the smell of cut leeks blew in from the fields, while on the horizon you could see the chimneys with their plumes of black smoke rising into the reddening sky. The red sky grew violet and then black and we could no longer see the broad, strong bands of smoke rising like the upward strokes of a paintbrush from the chimneys. The smell of leeks grew stronger, mixed with the bitter scent of onions. Far away behind the hollow of a sand pit lights were burning, and in front where the road passed, a man came by on a bicycle. The cone of light from his lamp moved jerkily over the rough surface. There was a clatter of loose screws, and the sound of the flapping mudguard faded away slowly and, one could almost say, solemnly. As I gazed, I saw up behind the road a wall, darker than the night sky, and behind it I heard the cackling of geese and the gentle, coaxing voice of a woman calling the birds to feed.

All I could see of Kate lying on the dark ground was her white face and the strange blue radiance of her eyes, when she opened them. Her arms, too, were white and bare and she was weeping bitterly. When I kissed her I could taste her tears. I felt dizzy. The dome of heaven swayed gently to and fro and Kate sobbed more and more vehemently.

We brushed the dirt off our clothes and walked slowly to the train terminal. Long before it came in, we heard the tram swinging round the curves and saw the sparks dripping from the overhead line.

"It's getting cold," said Kate.

"Yes, it is."

"Where are you sleeping tonight?"

"At the Blocks'."

We walked down the Blitzed avenue which leads to the tramway till we came to the pub by the station. We went in and sat down and I ordered two cognacs. Then I put a coin into the slot of the pinball machine, released the nickel balls into the wooden track, and fired them off one by one. They dodged round the steel obstacles, cannoned against the nickel contacts which rang softly as they touched them, while red, green, and blue numbers appeared successively on a glass dial. Kate and the landlady watched me and as I went on playing I laid my hand on Kate's head. The landlady was sitting with her arms crossed and a smile on her face. I went on playing and Kate watched me. A man came in and worked himself on to one of the bar stools, put his bag on a table behind him, and ordered a schnapps. His face was dirty and his hands brown and his china-blue eyes seemed brighter than they really were. He looked at my hand which was still resting on Kate's hair, then he looked at me and ordered another schnapps. Shortly after he got off the stool and started playing on the second automatic, an inconspicuous object looking rather like a cash register. It had a slot, a crank handle, and a glass plate on which there were three big black numbers in a line. The man put his coin into the slot and turned the handle. The numbers on the plate turned and vanished. Then one heard three crashes, one after another, and the number 146 appeared on the plate.

"Nothing," said the man and put in another coin. The plate with the numbers rushed round and one heard again the three separate crashes and then, after a moment of silence, some coins tumbled out of the steel nozzle of the machine.

"Four," said the man and smiled at me. "That's better."

Kate lifted my hand from her head and said, "I must go."

Outside a tram was swinging round the curve with screaming brakes. I paid for our drinks and took Kate to the tram stop. I kissed her as she got in and she stroked my cheek. The tram started and she waved to me till she was out of sight.

When I got back into the pub, I found the man with the grimy face still standing at the automatic machine, his hand on the handle. I ordered a cognac, lit a cigarette, and watched him. I thought I could recognize the rhythm when the dial with the numbers began to rotate and I got nervous when the final stop signal sounded, too soon, as it seemed to me, and I heard the man muttering, "Nothing—nothing—two nothing—nothing."

The pale face of the landlady was no longer smiling when the man left the pub with a curse. Then I changed some money and took his place at the machine ready to set the works in motion. I shall not soon forget the moment when I first pressed the lever down and set the glass dial revolving at full speed and when the three separate crashes came and I listened for the clink of coins—and nothing came out.

I stayed there nearly half an hour, drinking and working the machine, watching the whirling dial and listening to the brittle crashes. When I left the place I hadn't a penny left in my pocket and had to walk for three quarters of an hour to get to my lodging in the Blocks' house. Since then I only go to pubs which have such automatic machines. There I listen to the fascinating rhythm of the dial, wait for the crashes, and tremble with anxiety when the machine stops and nothing comes out.

The timing of our meetings is very irregular. They are usually sudden and unprepared. It often happens that, before I go to ground somewhere for the night, I visit our block and call Kate down by ringing the bell in a special way agreed on between us to prevent the children from knowing that I am in the neighborhood. The extraordinary thing is that they seem to love me and miss me and talk about me, although I used to beat them in the last weeks that I lived with them. I used to beat them cruelly and I remember how shocked I was to see my face, pale and covered with sweat, in the looking glass. And I remember covering my ears with my hands so as not to hear the cries of my boy, whom I had beaten for singing. Once on a Saturday afternoon Clemens and Carla caught me as I was waiting in the doorway below for Kate. I shrank when I saw an expression of joy suddenly appear on their faces at the sight of me. They tumbled over me, kissed me, and asked if I was well, and made me go upstairs with them. But as soon as I came into our room I felt chilled by the dreadful breath of poverty. Even the laughter of our little boy, who seemed to recognize me, and the joy of my wife at seeing me, could not banish that hateful feeling of irritation, which possessed me as soon as the children began to dance and sing. I left them to avoid flying into a rage.

But often when I am sitting in drinking shops I suddenly see their faces among the beer bottles and glasses, and I cannot forget the fright I got when I saw my children this morning walking in the Procession.

When I heard them singing the closing hymn in the cathedral, I sprang off the bed and opened the window from which I could see the scarlet figure of the bishop striding through the crowd.

Looking down, I saw the black hair of a woman leaning out of a window on the ground floor. She was wearing a dress covered with sequins and looked as if her head was on the window sill. Suddenly she turned and looked upward and I recognized the thin, greasy face of the landlady. "It's dinnertime, if you want to eat," she called out. "All right," I said, "I'm coming down."

As I went downstairs the toothpaste firm's cannon began to boom again.

KATE

The cake was baked to a turn. When I took it out of the oven, the warm, sweet smell of baking streamed into the room. The children were beaming. I sent Clemens to buy some cream, put it into a sprinkler and, to please the children, molded tendrils and circles on the damson-blue surface of the cake. I saw them eating what was left of the cream out of the basin and was glad to notice how accurately Clemens was sharing it. When, at last, there was one spoonful left over, he gave it to his baby brother who was sitting in his little chair and smiling at me as I washed my hands and put on my new lipstick.

"Are you going to be away for long?"

"Yes, till tomorrow morning."

"Is Papa coming back soon?"

"Yes."

My blouse and skirt were hanging on the kitchen cupboard. When I heard the young man whom I had engaged to look after the children coming in, I withdrew into the cubicle. This young fellow only gets a mark an hour for sitting in, but from four in the afternoon till seven in the morning is fifteen hours, which makes fifteen marks; and in addition he gets his food, and in the evening, when his vigil really begins, there have to be cigarettes waiting for him by the radio which the Hopfs have lent me.

Bellermann is his name. He seems to like the children. In any case they like him, and after my outings they always tell me about the games they have played with him and the stories he has told them. He was recommended to me by the chaplain and is clearly aware of my reasons for leaving the children and he raises his eyebrows slightly when he looks at my painted lips.

I put on my blouse, tidied my hair, and came out into the living room where I found that Bellermann had brought a gentle-faced, fair-haired girl with him. She had already taken the little boy in her arms and was twirling his rattle round her forefinger which seemed to amuse him. Bellermann introduced her to me but I did not catch her name. Her smile and her extraordinary gentleness with the child showed a sort of professional efficiency, and from the way in which she looked at me I could see she took me for an unnatural mother.

Bellermann has very short hair and a shiny skin and he is always screwing up his nose.

The girl said, "May we go out with the children?"

Clemens looked appealingly at me and Carla nodded in anticipation and of course I agreed. I went to get some money for chocolates out of the drawer but the girl refused to take it. "Please don't be cross," she said, "but if I may, I would like to pay for the chocolates myself."

"You may," I said, putting the money back. I felt pitiable in the presence of this blooming young creature.

"Let Gulli do what she wants," said Bellermann, "she is absolutely crazy about children."

I looked at my children in order—Clemens, Carla, and the little one—and felt my eyes filling with tears. Clemens smiled at me and said, "Off you go, Mummy. We shall be all right. We promise not to go to the water side."

"No, no," said Bellermann, and they both laughed.

Bellermann helped me into my cloak. I took my bag, kissed the children, and blessed them. I felt that I was redundant. I stopped for an instant outside the door, listened to them laughing inside, and went slowly down the stairs.

It was just half-past three and the streets were still empty. There were a few children playing hopscotch who looked up as I drew near. There was nothing to be heard in this street, which is inhabited by several hundred persons, except the sound of my footsteps. From far away came the dull strumming of a piano, and behind a curtain which was flapping slowly I saw an old woman with a yellow face holding an overfed mongrel in her arms. We have been living on this street for eight years, but when I look up, as I walk along, I always get giddy. Now the gray walls with their patches of dirt seemed to lean inward and along the narrow, gray strip of sky the thin tinkle of a piano floated. It seemed to me that the tones were not free and that the tune which a girl's pale fingers fumbled for and could not find was a broken melody. I hurried past the children who looked at me, I thought, threateningly.

Fred ought not to leave me alone. Although it makes me happy to meet him I am shocked by the fact that, in order to be with him, I have to leave the children. Whenever I ask him where he is living, he gives an evasive answer and I don't know these Blocks with whom he is supposed to have been lodging for the last month, nor will he give me their address. Sometimes we meet for a short half-hour in a café while the landlady of our block looks after the children. Then I have to go and we kiss hurriedly at the tram stop and Fred stands there and waves to me as I am carried away. There are nights when I lie on our divan bed and weep, while all around me is silence. I can hear the breathing of the elder children and the baby turning over. He is beginning to be restless as he is teething. I weep and pray as I hear the mills of time grinding dully on. I was twenty-three when we got married. Since then fifteen years have rolled by, without my noticing, but I have only to look at the faces of my children to know that every year which is added to their lives is taken away from mine.

At Tuckhoff Square I took the bus and, as we traveled, I looked out on to the quiet streets in which there was no one but an occasional man outside a tobacconist's. At Benekam Street I got out and went onto the porch of the Church of the Seven Sorrows to find out when there would be an evening service.

It was dark on the porch as I looked for matches in my bag, fumbling about among loose cigarettes, lipstick, handkerchiefs, and my washing things. At last I found a box and lit a match. I got a shock for there in a dark corner there was someone standing—someone who didn't move. I tried to say something like "Hello," but I could hardly speak for fear and the beating of my heart. The figure in the darkness did not stir. It was holding something in its hands which looked like a stick. The match burned out and I threw it away and lit another, but even when I saw that it was a statue my heart did not stop thumping. I took a step forward and perceived in the dim light that it was an angel with flowing hair and a lily in its hand. I leaned forward till my chin was almost touching its breast and looked long into the angel's face. The hair and face were thickly coated with dust and the blind eye sockets were filled with black fluff. I carefully blew them out and freed the gentle oval countenance from dust and then I suddenly realized that the smiling lips were made of plaster and that, by blowing away the dirt, I was blowing away the charm of the angel's smile. Still I went on blowing, cleaned up the luxuriant tresses and the breast and the billowing garments and tidied up the lily with short, sharp puffs of breath. But my pleasure in its beauty diminished as the garish colors became visible and the beastly varnish which the industry uses for religious statuary grew brighter. I turned away and walked further into the porch to look for the church notices. I lit a match and saw in the distance the soft red light of the lamp which is never put out. While I was standing by the black notice board I had another fright. This time a real person came up to me from behind. I turned round and sighed with relief when I recognized the pale, round, peasant's face of one of the priests. He stopped in front of me with an unhappy look on his face. My match went out and he asked me in the darkness what I was looking for.

"A mass," I said. "When can I go to mass this evening?"

"Holy mass will be celebrated in the cathedral at five o'clock."

I could only see his dull, fair hair and the glimmer of his tired eyes. Outside the trams were sweeping by and I heard the hoot of motors. Then I suddenly said into the darkness, "I want to confess."

I felt very much afraid, but relieved at the same time, to have got it out. Then the priest, who seemed to have been waiting for me to say it, said, "Come with me."

"No, here, please," said I.

"Impossible," he said gently, "in a quarter of an hour prayers will begin and people may come in. The confession box is inside the church." I would have liked to tell the priest everything on this dark, drafty porch in the presence of the stucco angel and with the distant red light to look at. I would have whispered my confession to him in the darkness and received a whispered absolution.

I followed him obediently into the courtyard, and the excitement which had filled me for a moment died away as we made our way between loose pieces of rubble and fragments of freestone from the walls of the church to the little gray house up against the wall of the tram depot.

Though it was Sunday afternoon one could hear metal being hammered inside. The door was opened by a house-keeper with a sulky face who sized me up with a sur-prised and suspicious expression.

It was dark in the hall and the priest said to me, "Wait a moment, please." From somewhere round a corner I heard the clatter of kitchen utensils and then I recognized the disagreeable sweetish smell which hung about the hall and clung to the damp walls. Warm fumes of boiling turnips floated round the corner from the kitchen. At last a light shone from one of the doorways opening on the hall and I recognized the shadow of the priest on the wall. "Come in," he called.

I hesitated and then went in. The room looked awful. There seemed to be a bed in a corner behind a reddish curtain. I thought I could smell it. There were book-shelves of various sizes in the walls and some of them were out of line. Round a huge table were a few valuable old chairs with black velvet backs, grouped at random. On the table there were books, a package of tobacco, cigarette papers, a bag full of carrots, and various news-papers. The priest stood behind the table. He beckoned me in and at the same time pushed forward a chair on the back of which a grating was nailed, slantwise to the table. I liked his face now that I saw it in the light.

"You must excuse us," he said with a look at the door and a gentle inclination of his head. "We are country folk and I can't persuade her not to boil turnips for soup. It costs much more than if we bought it in a tin, when one thinks of the price of coal, the dirt, the smell, and the work that goes into it, but I can't talk her out of it. Now come."

He pushed the chair with the grating nearer the table, sat down on it and beckoned to me. I went round the table and seated myself near him.

He then put on his stole and leaned his arms on the table. There was something studied and professional in the way in which he supported his head on his hand and covered his profile. Some of the squares in the grating were broken and when I began to whisper, "In the name of the Father, the Son, and the Holy Ghost," I saw him look at his wrist watch. I followed his glance and saw that it was three minutes past four. I began to speak. In a whisper I poured my fears, my sorrows, and the story of my life into his ear. I told him of my fear of pleasure, my fear of receiving the Blessed Sacrament, and of our restless married life. I told him that my husband had left me and that I only met him now and then, so that we could be together, and when I paused for a moment, he looked quickly at his watch and each time I followed his look and saw that the minute hand was moving on very slowly. Then he raised his eyelids and I saw his eyes and the yellow nicotine stains on his fingers. "Go on," he said, lowering his eyes again. He spoke gently and yet it hurt me to hear him, as it hurts when a skillful hand presses the matter out of a wound.

So I went on whispering into his ear and told him about the time, two years ago, when we both, Fred and I, drank too much. I told him about the death of my children, about my living ones, about what we have to hear through the wall from the Hopfs' room, and what they have heard from ours. Then I got stuck again. He looked once more at his watch and I saw that it was only six minutes after four. "Go on," he said gently. So I whispered on, speaking more quickly now, and told him how I hated the clergy who lived in great houses and had faces like advertisements for complexion cream. I told him about Mrs. Franke, about our inability to help ourselves, about the dirt in our home, and finally I told him that I was probably pregnant again.

When I came to a stop, he did not look at his watch but opened his eyes for half a second longer than usual and asked, "Is that all?" And I said, "Yes," and looked at his watch which was right in front of my eyes, as his hands, no longer covering his face, lay folded on the edge of the table. It was eleven minutes past four. I looked involuntarily into his loose, hanging sleeve and saw his hard, muscular arm with the shirt sleeve rolled up. I remember wondering why he kept his shirt sleeves like that.

He sighed and covered his face with his hands. Then he asked me softly, "Do you pray?" I said, "Yes," and told him that at night I often lie for hours on my shabby divan bed and say all the prayers I can think of and that

I sometimes light a candle so as not to wake the children by turning on the electric light and read to myself those prayers out of the prayer book that I don't know by heart.

He asked me no more questions and I kept silence, looking at the watch on his wrist. It was fourteen minutes past four. Outside I heard the noise of hammering in the tram depot, the cook singing in the kitchen and the throbbing of a tram in the railway station.

At last he took his hands from his face, folded them over his knees, and said, without looking at me, "In the world ye have fear, but be ye comforted. I have overcome the world. Can you understand that?"

Without waiting for my answer he continued, "Go ye through the narrow door, for wide is the gate and broad the way which leads to destruction and many are they that enter therein. How strait is the gate and how narrow the way that lead to life and how few are they that find them!"

After another silence he covered his face with his hands again and murmured between his fingers, "Narrow, yes, the narrowest path we know is that which leads along the blade of a knife, and I think that is the path you are treading." And suddenly he put his hands down and looked at me for a second through the openings in the grating. I shrank before the sternness of his eyes which before had seemed so kindly. Then he said, "I command you to go and hear the holy mass said by your parish priest, whom you hate so much, and to receive the holy communion from his hands when"—and he looked at me again—"when you have received absolution."

He fell silent again and seemed to be pondering; and

while I was trying to say to myself all the prayers and penitential texts which I knew, I could hear the hissing of the welding torches in the depot and suddenly the church clock struck the quarter.

"I don't know if I can absolve you," he said. "We must wait." Then he added vehemently, "Good heavens! How can you hate so bitterly?" Then he made a gesture of helplessness and turned to me saying, "I can bless you—but you must excuse me, I have to think it over and perhaps I ought to consult a colleague. Can you come this evening? No, of course, you are meeting your husband. You must see to it that he comes back to you."

I was very sad because he would not absolve me and I said, "I beg you to grant me absolution." He smiled, and raised his hand slightly saying, "I wish I could, since you wish it so much, but I really am in doubt. Do you still feel hatred?" "Oh, no," I said hastily, "only sadness." He seemed to hesitate and I did not know what I ought to do. If I had gone on pressing him, he would, perhaps, have done it, but I wanted to be absolved properly and not to talk him into it.

Then he smiled again and said, "Conditionally—that is if I have the power to do so—and I feel so uncertain about that—I can absolve you." He fidgeted with his hands impatiently before my face and said, "You are allowing hatred to govern your judgment of others. We are not allowed to judge or to hate." He shook his head violently then laid it on his open hands on the edge of the table and prayed. Then he stood up quickly and gave me absolution. I crossed myself and stood up. He stood by the table and looked at me and, suddenly, before he began to speak, I pitied him.

"I can only . . ." then he seemed to wipe the words away with a movement of his hand. "Do you think that I, a priest, do not feel hatred? I feel it here," and he tapped his black cassock below the region of his heart. "Sometimes I hate my religious superiors. Here," and he pointed to the window, "in my church the masses are said by priests passing through our city. They come from the hotels in the neighborhood, well-groomed men going to conferences or coming from them and they grumble about the dirt and the lack of servers. Here the ten-minute, the thirteen-minute, the twenty-minute and the normal five- and twenty-minute masses are said. That means five, ten, and often fifteen masses a day. You wouldn't believe how many of the clergy pass through. Some are going to health resorts and others coming from them—and there are conferences enough, goodness knows! Think of fifteen services at which altogether hardly five worshipers are present. That beats all records for small congregations. It sounds like long odds on the totalizer! Oh! Why should I hate them, these poor priests who leave an exquisite smell of hotel bath salts in my tumble-down sacristy?" He turned back from the window and handed me a writing block and a pencil from the table. I wrote down my name and address and straightened my hat that had slipped to one side.

At this moment we heard a loud knocking on the door. "Yes, yes," he called, "I know it is time for service. I am coming."

He shook my hand in farewell, gazed at me with a sigh, and took me to the door.

I went slowly past the porch of the church to the subway. Two women and a man were going to the afternoon service. Opposite the church hung a great white streamer bearing in red letters the words, "What Are You Without Your Druggist?"

The sun had just emerged from the edge of a black cloud and its disk coincided exactly with the capital O in "Without" and filled it with yellow light. I went on my way. A boy with a prayer book under his arm passed me, and after that I was alone in the street which ran between ruined houses and shanties. From behind the burned-out frontages I heard the din from the depot. I smelled the warm fragrance of fresh baking and stopped. I turned to the right and looked into the door of a wooden shanty from which steam was floating in soft wreaths. On the threshold a child was sitting in the sun, blinking up at the sky. He had the gentle expression of an idiot. His eyelids were red and looked transparent in the sunlight. I felt sorry for the little chap. He had a fresh doughnut in his hand. There were smears of sugar round his mouth and when he bit into the doughnut some brownish jam oozed out and dropped on his pullover. Inside I saw a girl bending over a copper. Her face was beautiful and she had a skin as smooth as a bulb and though her hair was covered with a kerchief I could see that she must be blonde. She was fishing the fresh-baked doughnuts out of the steaming lard and laying them on a grid, when suddenly she raised her eyes and smiled at me.

Her smile fell on me like a charm and I smiled back and for some seconds we stood there motionless. Of course I could only see her really, but I seemed to see myself too from far off, and I felt I was looking at the mirage of the two of us smiling at one another like sisters. Then I dropped my eyes, for I remembered that I had no money with me to buy one of her doughnuts, the smell of which had sharpened my appetite. I looked at the idiot's pale blond mop of hair and was sorry that I had put no money in my purse. I never take money with me when I go to meet Fred, because he can't resist the sight of it and generally makes me waste it on drink for the pair of us. I saw the idiot-boy's fat neck and the crumbs of sugar scattered over his face and something like envy possessed me when I looked at his soft, open lips.

When I looked up again I saw that the girl had pushed the copper on one side. She was just untying the scarf from her head and her hair streamed down with the sunshine on it. And again I saw not only her but myself as if from a height, and there was the dingy street lined with ruins, the church porch, the streamer with the advertisement, and myself standing at the entrance of the shanty—myself thin and sad but smiling.

I walked carefully past the boy into the shanty. In a corner two children were sitting at a table and near the stove was an old unshaven man who lowered his newspaper and looked at me.

The girl who was standing near the coffee machine looked into the glass and tidied her hair. I looked at her small, white, childish hands and saw in the mirror along-side her fresh and smiling face my own—thin and sallow, lit by the narrow, lambent flame of my dark red mouth. The smile on my face, though it came from my heart and almost against my will, seemed false, and now in my fancy our heads seemed to change places. She had my head and I had hers, and I saw myself as a young girl standing before the glass tidying my hair. And I thought of this girl giving herself to a man whom she would love and who would pour life and death into her and leave on her face the imprint of the thing he called love, until it grew to resemble mine—haggard and sallow from the bitterness of life.

But now she turned round, covering my image in the glass, and I stepped to the right and let myself enjoy her charm.

"Good afternoon," I said.

"Good afternoon. Would you like some doughnuts?"

"No, thank you."

"Oh, why? Don't they smell good?"

"Indeed they do," I said and shuddered at the thought of the unknown man to whom she would belong. "Very good, but I have no money with me."

When I said the word "money" the old man by the stove stood up and went behind the counter. Then he stood by the girl and said, "Money? But you can pay later. You would like some doughnuts, wouldn't you?"

"I would," I said.

"Oh, please sit down," said the girl.

I went and sat down at a table near the two children.

"You'll have coffee too?" asked the girl.

"Yes, please."

The old man heaped three cakes on to a plate and brought them to me. He remained standing near me.

I said to him, "Many thanks, but you do not know me."

He smiled at me and unclasped his hands from behind his back and laid them clumsily on his belly murmuring, "I am not anxious." I nodded toward the idiot who was still sitting on the threshold and said, "Is he your son?"

"Yes," he said softly, "he is my son and she is my daughter." As he spoke he glanced at the girl behind the counter who was working the handle of the coffee machine.

"He doesn't understand the speech of human beings, my son doesn't," said the old man, "or the language of animals, for that matter. He can't say a single word— only *tzoo-tza-tzeh* and we can't imitate him properly. We say *tsoo-tsa-tseh*." He had put out his tongue to pronounce these sounds. "We haven't the knack," he went on gently. Then raising his voice a little, he called out suddenly, "Bernard," and the idiot turned his head clumsily and then let it fall forward again. Once more the old man called, "Bernard," and the boy turned toward him and then his head swung back like a pendulum. The old man got up, took the child gently by the hand, and led him to my table. He sat down by me on a chair and took his son on his lap. Then he said to me quietly, "But perhaps it upsets you to have him near you. Don't mind saying so, if it does."

"Oh, no," I said, "it doesn't upset me." Then his

daughter brought a cup of coffee and put it in front of me. She remained standing by her father. "You must say so, if it bothers you," she said. "It would not annoy us. Most people don't like it."

The child was fat and his face was greasy. He looked dully in front of him and drooled his *tzoo-tza-tzeh*. I looked at him attentively and, raising my head, I said, "No, he does not upset me at all. He's like a baby in arms." I put the cup to my lips, drank some coffee, and took a mouthful of doughnut. "How good your coffee is!" I said. "Really?" said the girl. "Do you really think so? That is what a man said to me this morning and he was the first person who ever said it."

"Yes, it's awfully good," I said, and drank again and went on with my doughnut. The girl leaned against the back of her father's chair, looked at me, and then, gazing over my head, said, "Sometimes I try to imagine what he feels and how he lives. He is generally so peaceful and happy. Maybe he can only see two colors—green and brown, for instance. Perhaps the air seems like water to him, green water, because he can only move through it slowly—green water which sometimes darkens into brown, striped with blackish lines like an old film. Sometimes he cries when he hears certain noises like the grinding of the tramcars and the tooting on the wireless —when that comes, he weeps and it is dreadful."

"Oh," I said, "he cries, does he?"

"Oh, yes," she answered and looked at me again, this time without smiling, "he often cries and he always does when he hears these shrill sounds. Then he weeps bitterly and the tears run down into the smears round his mouth. The only things he can eat are sweets, milk, and bread. He can't keep anything else down. Oh, forgive me," she said, "I have disgusted you."

"No, no," I said. "Go on telling me."

She looked past me again and laid her hand on the child's head. "I think that just as he finds it hard to move his body against the flow of the air, so he finds these particular sounds terrifying. Perhaps his ear is always full of soft organ sounds, a sort of dark brown tune which he alone can hear. Perhaps he hears a storm roaring through invisible trees. Or maybe he hears the thrumming of strings as thick as your arm—a buzzing which calls him and which is shattered by these high notes."

While she spoke the old man listened to her as if entranced, holding his hands round the body of the child, heedless of the sugar and jam that dripped on to his coat sleeve. I drank some more coffee and began my second doughnut. Then I asked the girl softly, "How do you know all this?"

She looked at me smiling and said, "Oh, I don't know it, but perhaps—anyhow there must be something inside him, which we don't know, and I try to imagine what it is. Sometimes, too, he suddenly starts screaming—suddenly, without warning. Then he comes running to me and I let him cry into my apron. Sometimes this happens when he is sitting by the door and I think to myself that he must suddenly, just for half a second, have perceived things just as we do—people, motors, trams, and all the noise—and the sight terrified him. Then he cries for a long time."

The children who had been sitting in the corner got up, pushed their plates away, and walked by us on their way out. A pert little girl with a green cap called, "Mother said to put it down."

"Yes, that's all right," said the old man and smiled at them.

I asked him if his wife, the boy's mother, was dead. "Yes," he said, "she is dead. A bomb tore her to pieces in the street. The child was blown out of her arms and landed on a bale of straw and was found crying there."

"Was he like this since his birth?"

"Yes," said the girl, "he has always been like this. He takes no notice of anything. The only things which seem to reach him are our voices, when we call him by name, the organ in the church, the screaming sound of the trams, and the monks chanting the litany. But do go on eating—or are you disgusted after all?"

I took the last doughnut, shook my head, and said, "Did you say that he hears the monks?"

"Yes," she said quietly, "I think he must hear them. When I take him to the convent church—in Bildoner Square, you know—for the choral service, his face changes and seems to shrink and his expression becomes stern. It always frightens me. He listens and I know he hears. He is quite different then. He hears the sound of the chanting and when the monks stop he weeps. You find that strange?" she added smiling. "Go on with your doughnut."

I took up the doughnut again and bit into it and felt the warm jam flowing into my mouth.

"I suppose you often take him to Bildoner Square."

"Oh, yes," she said, "I often go with him there although it frightens me to see him like that. Will you have some more coffee?"

"No, thanks. I have to go." I looked hesitatingly at her and the idiot and said softly, "I would like to see that."

"You mean in the convent church?"

"Yes," I said.

"Oh, then do come. It's a pity you are going now. You'll come back, won't you?"

"Of course I'll come back. I still have to pay for my coffee."

"Oh, not for that. But do come again."

The old man nodded agreement. I drank the last mouthful of coffee, got up, and shook the crumbs of doughnut from my cloak.

"Yes, I'll come again. It's so nice here."

"Will you come today?" asked the girl.

"No, not today. Perhaps tomorrow morning. I'll come often and we'll go together to the monks."

"Yes, we will," she said. She gave me her slender white hand which I held for a moment as I looked smiling into her flowerlike face. Then I nodded to the old man and said, "Bernard," in a soft voice to the idiot, who was crumbling a cake in his fingers, but he did not hear me and seemed not to see me. His red, inflamed eyelids were almost closed.

I turned round and went along to the dark subway which leads to Station Street.

FRED

When I came down I found plates being carried in piles from the tables. There was a smell of cold goulash, salad, and artificially sweetened pudding. I took a seat at a corner table and saw two young fellows standing by a pinball machine and playing. The clear tinkle of the nickel balls touching the contacts, the numbers rushing by on the dial, and the final crash excited me. The waiter was brushing the crumbs off the table with a napkin and the skinny landlady was nailing a yellow cardboard square on the counter on which was written, "Dancing Tonight. Entrance Free."

At the table next to me was sitting an old man, in a

tweed overcoat and a Tyrolese hat, whose pipe was smoking in an ashtray. The man, who was wearing his green hat, was poking about in his plate of goulash.

"What may I serve you?" said the waiter.

I looked at him and it seemed to me that his face was familiar.

"What is there?"

"Goulash," he said, "pork chops, potatoes, salad, sweet. Or you can start with soup, if you wish.

"I'll have soup and goulash to follow. And give me a rye whisky."

"Very good," said the waiter.

The food was plentiful and hot and I perceived that I was hungry. I helped myself to bread and dabbed it in the sharply spiced sauce. Afterward I ordered another rye. The young fellows were still playing the pinball machine; one of them had his hair standing straight up like a crest.

I paid for my meal and waited for a few minutes but the machines were not yet free. I looked once more closely at the waiter. I must have seen that pale face and whitish hair somewhere.

I got some cigarettes at the counter and the landlady looked at me and said, "Are you going to stay the whole night?"

I said I was.

"In that case would you mind paying in advance?" she said with a smirk. "We find it safer so near the railway station. And you have no luggage."

"Oh, yes, of course," I said and took some money out of my wallet.

"Eight marks, please," she said and licked the point of her pencil before writing me a receipt.

"Are you waiting for someone?" she asked as she gave me the paper.

"Yes, my wife."

"Oh, all right," said she as she handed me a package of cigarettes. I put a mark on the counter and went upstairs.

I lay for a long time on the bed ruminating and smoking without knowing exactly what I was puzzling over, when it occurred to me that I was trying to make out who the waiter's face belonged to. I never forget faces. They follow me about and I recognize them as soon as they bob up again. They paddle about in my subconscious, especially those which I have only once seen, and swim around like shadowy gray fish between clumps of seaweed in a cloudy pool. Sometimes they push their heads hard against the surface and in the end their identity always comes through when I see them again. I restlessly tried to catch my fish in this pool full of faces, then I flicked up my hook and there was the waiter, last seen when he was lying next me in a casualty clearing station for a few minutes. Then the lice were creeping out of the bandage round his head and feasting on his fresh blood and the drying blood of his wound. Some of them were crawling quietly up his neck and into his thin, whitish hair, and others moved over the face of the unconscious man and adventurously climbed up his ears

108

and then slipped off and caught on his shoulders from where they vanished eventually in his dirty collar band. Yes, that was how I had seen that narrow, unhappy face two thousand miles away, and now its owner was carelessly helping me to goulash. I was glad when I had placed him. Then I turned on one side, took my money out of my pocket, and counted it on the pillow. I still had sixteen marks and eighty pfennigs.

Then I went down to the saloon, but found the pinball machine still occupied by the same two young men. One of them seemed to have acquired a pocket full of coins. His jacket hung down heavily on one side and he raked about with his right hand among the change.

The man in the green hat was still there drinking beer and reading a newspaper. I drank a schnapps and looked at the well-greased face of the landlady who was sitting on a stool turning over the leaves of an illustrated paper. I went upstairs and lay down on the bed. As I lay and smoked I started thinking about Kate and the children and the war and the twins who, the priests assure me, are now in heaven. Every day I think of these two children, but today they filled my mind for a long time. No one who knows me, hardly even Kate, would have believed how often I think of them. Everyone thinks of me as an unstable character, who has changed his job every three years since he ran through the money his father left him, who doesn't become steadier as he grows older, who cares little about his family, and who gets drunk as often as he can afford to.

But in reality it is very seldom that I drink too much—

not once a month—and I don't get properly plastered more than once every three months. Sometimes I ask myself what people think I do on the twenty-nine days of the month when I don't drink. Well, as a matter of fact, I walk a great deal, I try to earn money in my spare time by selling what remains of my schoolboy knowledge to backward youngsters. I roam through the town and often wander out into the suburbs and visit the cemeteries when they are open. There I walk between well-tended hedges and tidy flower beds and read the names on the tombstones and breathe into my nostrils the smell of the graveyard and feel my heart fluttering when I think that I, too, will be lying there some day. Formerly, when we still had money, we used to travel a lot, but I used to do the same things in strange towns as I now do here, where I expect to remain. I often used to lie on my bed in the hotels where we stayed. I smoked a lot and went for aimless walks, now and then going into a church, and I often wandered out into the suburbs where the cemeteries are. I used to drink in third-class pubs and fraternize by night with strangers whom I knew I would never see again. Even as a child I used to like going to cemeteries, indulging a passion supposed to be unnatural in young people. But all these names, these graveyard borders, every letter on a headstone, the smell of decay—everything tells me that I too must die and that is for me the only certainty. Often among the endless lines of graves by which I walk, I discover the names of people whom I have known.

While I was still a child I learned what death is. My

mother died when I was seven and I noticed everything that happened to her. The priest came and anointed her and blessed her. She lay still and did not move. Flowers were brought to her room, and a coffin. Relatives came and wept and prayed at her beside. She lay still and did not move. In my curiosity I followed all that happened. I was slapped for watching the undertaker's men at their work. They washed my mother and clothed her in a white shift, arranged the flowers round her coffin, nailed down the lid, carried the coffin down, and placed it on a motor hearse. And the house was empty. My mother was not there. Then, without my father's knowledge, I went to the cemetery. I took a Number 12 bus—how well I remember it all!—changed at Tuckhoff Square into a Number 10 and rode to the end of the line. Then I set foot in a cemetery for the first time. There was a man wearing a green hat at the gate. I asked him about my mother. He had a bloated red face and smelled of wine. He took me by the hand and went across with me to the office. He was very kind and asked my name. Then he took me into a room and told me to wait. I waited. I walked between the chairs round a light brown table, looked at the pictures on the wall, and waited. One of the pictures was of a small, slender woman, sitting on an island and waiting. I stood on tiptoe and tried to read what was written on the frame and made out the word, "Nana." Another picture showed a bearded man leering into a mug of beer with a richly ornamented lid which he was raising to his mouth. I couldn't read the inscription. I went to the door, but I could not open it. Then I sat down

on one of the yellow wooden chairs and cried until I
heard steps in the passage outside. It was my father. I
knew his footsteps from hearing them so often in the
hall at home. Father was kind to me and we went with the
fat man in the green hat, who smelled of wine, into the
mortuary, and there I saw a lot of coffins with names and
numbers, and my father touched one of the nameplates
with his finger and read out to me "Elizabeth Bogner—
18-4-16.00 hrs—Lot VII/4." He asked me what the date
was. I did not know and he said it was the sixteenth.
"Mother won't be buried till the day after tomorrow,"
he said. I made him promise that they would not do anything to the coffin without my seeing it, and my father
cried and promised. Then I went with him to our dark
house and helped him to clear out the large, old-
fashioned storeroom. There we brought to light things
which Mother had bought from peddlers over many
years: heaps of rusty razor blades, stacks of soap, insect
powder, half-perished elastic bands, and many boxes full
of safety pins. My father wept.

Two days later I saw the coffin again. It looked the
same as before. They loaded it on to a cart and covered
it with wreaths and bunches of flowers. We followed
the priest and the acolytes till we came to a great clayey
hole on Lot VII. There I saw them bless the coffin, lower
it into the pit, sprinkle it with holy water, and throw a
handful of earth on it. And I listened to the priest praying and speaking of dust—of dust and resurrection.

We stayed a long time in the cemetery, my father and
I, because I insisted on seeing everything. The grave-
diggers filled the grave with earth, stamped it down, and

then built up a little mound with their spades. They laid the wreaths on the top of it and finally one of them stuck a small white wooden cross into the mound. On it was written in black letters which I was able to read "Elizabeth Bogner."

Even as a child I thought I knew exactly what death was. One went away, was buried in the earth, and lay waiting for the resurrection. I understood the idea very well and concluded that everyone must die. Many persons whom I knew died, and they could not keep me from going to the funerals.

Perhaps thinking about death is my chief vice, and the people who condemn me as a drinker judge me wrongly. Everything that I start soon becomes uninteresting, boring, and objectless; and since I have been living apart from Kate and the children, I have begun once more to frequent cemeteries. I try to get there early enough to be present at burials. I follow the coffins of unknown individuals, listen to grave-side speeches, join in the responses when the priest mumbles the words of the burial service over the open grave, throw earth on the coffin, and, if I have any money, buy a few flowers and drop them one by one on the loose soil which has been heaped over the coffin. I walk past the weeping relatives and it has happened that I have been invited to funeral feasts. There I have sat at table with strangers, drunk beer, and eaten potato salad and sausages and allowed weeping women to pile my plate with great slices of meat. I have smoked cigarettes and drunk schnapps with the mourners and have listened to the life stories of people of whom I knew nothing except

113

their coffins. I have been shown their photos, too; and a week ago I followed the coffin of a young woman and afterward sat in the corner of an old-fashioned restaurant beside her father, who took me for one of his daughter's secret lovers. He showed me pictures of her. She must have been a really beautiful creature. In one of the photos she was sitting with blown-back hair in a motor scooter at the entrance to an avenue. "She was still a child," said her father to me, "and had not yet known love." I had strewed flowers on her coffin and now I saw tears in her father's eyes as he laid his cigarette in a gray earthenware ashtray and wiped them away.

I showed no zeal in any of the many different professions into which I ventured. I could not muster up the earnestness one needs to do a job properly. Before the war I was for some time in a pharmaceutical concern, but boredom overtook me and I went into a photography business and soon became sick of it. Then I wanted to be a librarian, though I never was fond of reading, and it was then that I met Kate, who loves books. I stayed on in the library because Kate was there, but we soon got married and she had to leave when she was going to have her first child. Then came the war and Clemens was born just when I had to join up.

I did not care to think about the war, so I got up and went down again to the bar. It was nearly four o'clock. I had a drink and went to the pinball machine, but when I had put in one coin and set the ball rolling, I felt very tired and went back to the bedroom, where I lay down again smoking and thinking of Kate till I heard the chimes from the Church of the Seven Sorrows.

KATE

I found the signpost with the black hand at once and
followed the direction in which the finger pointed. The
street was gray and empty but suddenly a lot of people
streamed out of a narrow building and I saw they were
coming from a cinema. At the corner of the street there
was another signpost showing a black hand with the
index finger extended; I saw that I was standing opposite
the hotel called Holland Court. I hesitated because the
house looked so dirty, but then I crossed the street slowly
and stopped in front of the red-painted revolving door.
After a moment's uncertainty I pushed through the door
and walked into the restaurant. There were three men
standing at the counter. As I came in, they looked at me

and stopped talking. Then they looked at the landlady and she raised her eyes from her magazine and saw me. She looked at my face and my hat and then at the bag I was carrying. Then she bent forward a little to get a glimpse of my shoes and my legs, and then she looked at my face once more and stared intently at my lips, as if she wished to make out what brand of lipstick I used. Then, leaning forward again and gazing at my legs, she said, "Yes?" As she did so, she took her hands from her hips and put them on the nickel counter. Then she clasped them over her stomach and her thin, white face assumed a helpless expression.

"I wish to go to my husband," I said, and the men turned away and began to talk to one another. Then the landlady, without waiting for me to tell her my name, said, "Number eleven, first floor." She pointed to the swinging door by the counter. One of the men sprang to the door and held it open for me. He was pale and seemed to be drunk. His lips trembled and the whites of his eyes were bloodshot. He lowered his eyes when I looked at him and said, "Thank you." Then I went through the door and, as I was going up the stairs, I heard through the swinging door a voice saying, "But she comes from here."

The banisters were painted green and behind the opaque glass windows one could see the black shadow of a wall. In the passage on the first floor a bare electric bulb was burning. I knocked at the door of Number 11 and, as there was no answer, I opened it and walked in. Fred was lying asleep on the bed. He looks very delicate and almost like a child lying in bed. One could take him for a lad of eighteen, if it wasn't for his tired face. He sleeps with slightly parted lips and his dark hair hanging over his forehead. His face shows complete unconsciousness—he sleeps very deeply. Going up the stairs I had felt angry with him, for he had forced me into a situation in which people took me for a whore; but now I went up to his bed very quietly, drew up a chair, and took a packet of cigarettes out of my bag.

I sat by his bed smoking and turned my eyes away from him when he began to be restless. I looked at the green, heart-shaped pattern of the wallpaper and the hideous lamp and blew the smoke of my cigarette toward the open window. I recalled the past and recognized that there had not been much change since our marriage. When the war broke out, we had just got into a proper home of our own, but I cannot believe it was ever real. Four rooms, a bathroom, and everything clean and tidy. Clemens had a Max-and-Moritz wallpaper, although he was too small to understand pictures. When he was big enough to understand them, the house with the Max-and-Moritz wallpaper no longer existed. I can still see Fred with his hands in the pockets of his gray uniform looking at the heap of rubble from which a wisp of gray smoke was softly rising. Fred didn't seem to grasp or feel our loss. He could not realize that we no longer had any linen, any furniture, or any other possessions. He looked at me like a man who had never really had anything of his own. He took the lighted cigarette out of his mouth and put it in mine. I drew in the smoke and blew it out in a violent burst of laughter.

I opened the window wide and threw the butt of my cigarette down into the courtyard. Between the rubbish bins there was a big puddle stained yellow with the ashes of burned-out briquettes. My cigarette dropped hissing into it. A train rolled into the station and I heard the voice of the loud-speaker without understanding a word that was said.

Fred awoke as the bells of the cathedral began to ring. The chimes made the windows vibrate and the vibration spread to a metal hook attached to the shutters on the window sill, which buzzed with the sound waves.

Fred looked at me without moving or speaking and I knew that he was coming slowly back to life.

"Fred," I said.

"Yes," he answered and drew me slowly down to him and kissed me. We embraced one another, gazed at one another, and when he took my head in his hands and held it away from him to look at me, I couldn't help laughing.

"We must go to mass," I said, "or have you already been?"

"No. I was only there for five minutes. I came for the blessing."

"Come then."

He had been lying down with his shoes on and had obviously fallen asleep without putting anything over himself and I saw that he was very cold. He poured some water into the basin and splashed his face with his hands. Then he dried himself and took his overcoat from the chair. We went arm in arm down the stairs. The three men were still standing by the counter talking to one another. They did not look at us. Fred gave the landlady the key of our room. She hung it on a board and asked, "Will you be long away?"

"An hour," said Fred.

When we got to the cathedral the Office was just finished, but we arrived in time to see the canons march slowly into the sacristy. They looked for all the world like a shoal of carp swimming slowly through clear gray water. A tired-looking priest said the mass at a side altar. He said it fast and seemed in a hurry, and he shrugged his shoulders impatiently when he went to read the Gospel on the left side of the altar and found that the server was not yet there. Clouds of incense floated from the high altar and many people, mostly wearing little red flags in their buttonholes, wandered round the group of worshipers who had come to attend the mass. At the moment of the Consecration some of these people halted out of reverence when they heard the bell, but most of them wandered on, gazing at the mosaics and the stained-glass windows, and went up to look at the different altars in the side chapels. When we went in, I had looked at the clock by the organ which chimes the quarters in a clear, soft tone. I looked again when we went out after the blessing and saw that the mass had lasted exactly nineteen minutes. Fred waited for me by the revolving door while I went to the altar of the Mother of God and said an *Ave*. I prayed not to be pregnant, though I knew I ought not to. Many candles were burning before the picture of the

Mother of God, and on the left of the great iron candelabra lay a bundle of yellow tapers. By it they had stuck up a cardboard square on which was written "An Offering from the Catholic Branch of the German Union of Druggists."

I rejoined Fred and we went out to find the sun shining. It was twenty past five and I was hungry. I clung to Fred's arm as we went down the broad terrace steps and heard him fingering the money in his pocket.

"Would you like to eat in a restaurant?" he asked.

"No," I said, "let us go to a snack bar. I like eating in snack bars."

"Come along then," he said, and we turned into Blücher Lane. Here the lapse of time has turned the heaps of ruins into little hills with rounded contours. On them weeds grow in profusion and gray-green undergrowth with a faint reddish sheen, the color of faded wild roses. For some time the Blücher monument had lain there in the gutter, a huge, muscular bronze figure looking furiously at the sky. But one day it was stolen.

Behind the wrought-iron gate the rubbish had piled up. There was only a narrow path kept open between the ruins. We followed this and when we came to Mommsen Street where there are a few houses still standing, I heard in the distance on the other side of the mounds of rubble the music of a merry-go-round. I held on to Fred and, as we stood there, I heard it more clearly: the blaring tones of an orchestrion.

I asked Fred if there was a fun fair in the town.

"Yes," he said, "I think so. They have got it up for the druggists. Shall we go and see?"

"Oh, yes, do let us," I said.

We quickened our steps, hurried through Veleda Street, and when we got round the corner we found ourselves in the middle of the noises and smells of the fair. The sound of barrel organs, the strong, spicy smell of goulash mixed with the sweetish odor of cakes baking in drippings, and the clear rushing music of the merry-go-round filled me with excitement. I felt my heart beating faster in the medley of smells and sounds through which, for all their confusion, I seemed to hear a hidden melody.

"Fred," I said, "give me some money."

He took the loose money out of his pocket separating the cash from the notes, which he folded and stuck into a shabby little pocketbook. He poured all the coins into my hand. There were some thick silver pieces in the heap. I counted it carefully while Fred looked at me smiling.

"Six marks eighty," I said. "That's too much, Fred."

"Please take it," he said, and I looked into his pale, thin, tired face and saw the snow-white cigarette between his bloodless lips and knew that I loved him. I have often asked myself why I love him and I don't know the answer exactly. There are many reasons, but one of them I do know. It is because it is lovely to be taken out by Fred.

"But you are my guest for supper," he said.

"As you like," I answered. I took his arm and drew him across to a booth where they served goulash. The front of the booth was decorated with painted Hungarian dancing girls, interspersed with peasant lads in round hats with their hands on their hips leaping about round the dancers. We leaned our arms on the counter and a woman who was sitting on a folding stool by a steaming cooking pot got up and came over to us with a smile. She was fat and black-haired and wore on her big, well-shaped hands a lot of cheap rings. Round her brownish neck she had a black velvet band with a medallion swinging from it.

"Two goulashes," I said and pushed two marks across to her. We smiled at one another, Fred and I, as the woman went back and took the lid off the pot.

"I've already eaten goulash once today," said Fred.

"Oh, I'm so sorry."

"Never mind," he said, "I'm fond of goulash," and he laid his hand on my arm.

The woman dipped deep into her caldron and dug out great spoonfuls of food. The steam which poured out of the cooking pot misted the looking glass on the wall behind the counter. She handed each of us a roll and then wiped the steam off the glass with a cloth, saying, "So that you may see how beautiful you are." I looked into the mirror and saw that I was really looking beautiful. Far in the background behind my face I saw the misty outline of a shooting gallery and behind it, to one side, was the contraption they call a chairoplane. I had a shock when I saw Fred's face in the glass. He can't eat hot food which hurts his sore gums, and he has to roll it round in his mouth till it cools. The expression of discouragement and impatience which he feels makes him look like a mumbling old man—and every time I see him like that it frightens me more. But the mirror clouded over once more as the woman raked round with her spoon and it seemed to me that she was giving the people standing by us smaller helpings than we had had.

When we had finished we pushed the empty plates back, thanked the woman, and went. I took Fred's arm again and we strolled slowly between the booths. I shot with an air gun at stiffly smiling puppets and was happy when I hit one of them in the head and saw it tumble back against the brown sackcloth behind, to be thrown back into its place by invisible machinery. Then I let myself be beguiled by the droning voice of the man in charge into buying a lottery ticket. I watched the wheel of fortune turning and threw a longing glance at the teddy bear which I hoped to win and which, since my childhood, I have been hoping to win. The noisy wheel revolved more and more slowly through the cogs till at last it stopped just before reaching my number. I did not win the teddy bear. I won nothing. After that I climbed into one of the narrow seats of the chairoplane and pressed two pennies into the dirty hand of an attendant. Then I was carried up gradually higher and higher, revolving round the orchestrion which was hidden in the belly of a wooden structure and which hurled its wild tunes into my face. I saw the cathedral tower flying by me far away over the ruins with their thick coat of weeds; I saw the roofs of the tents with puddles of rain water standing on them and, as I whirled round on my twopenny ride, I kept flying into the sunlight, which struck me like a blow whenever I came into it. I heard the grinding sound of the chains on which the chairs swung out and the shrieks of the women riders. I saw steam and eddies of dust rising from the fair, and chased round through the air that smelled of grease and sugar. At last when I tumbled down the steps which led down to the ground, I fell into Fred's arms crying, "Oh, Fred."

Then we went and danced together on a wooden stage. It cost us a penny each. In a crowd of teen-agers swaying from the hips, we moved closely locked together and, each time we turned in time with the music, I looked into the fat, lewd face of a trumpeter, whose dirty collar was half hidden by his instrument. He winked at me and blew piercing notes out of his trumpet which I thought were specially aimed at me.

Then I watched Fred playing roulette and marked the dumb excitement of the bystanders when the croupier set the wheel in motion and the ball began to dance. The speed with which they staked their money and Fred threw his pennies on to the squares he fancied seemed to me to imply a degree of familiarity and understanding which I had never guessed at. I saw how the good-looking little croupier raised his head while the ball was rolling round the board, and surveyed the scene with a cold, contemptuous glance. He did not lower his eyes till the rattle of the ball got fainter. When it ceased, as the ball came to rest, he raked in the losing stakes and put them in his pocket and then paid the winners.

Then he fumbled among the coins in his pocket and called on the players to make their stakes, watched the fingers of the people standing about the table and sent the board spinning round with a contemptuous gesture, lifting his head and pursing his lips and looking more bored than ever.

Fred twice won a heap of pennies. Then he took his money from the table and worked his way through the crowd till he came to me.

We sat down on the dirty steps of a show booth, tented in blue canvas, looked at the bustling crowds, and swallowed dust as we listened to the confused strains of the orchestrion and the harsh cries of the attendant as he took in the money. I looked at the ground and saw that it was covered with dirt, bits of paper, cigarette ends, trampled flowers, and torn tickets; and as I slowly raised my head I saw our children. Bellermann was holding Clemens' hand and the girl Carla's and the little boy was in the basket which Bellermann and the girl were carrying between them. The children had big, yellow sticks of candy in their mouths. I saw them laughing and looking about them. They stopped by the shooting gallery and Bellermann went up to the counter while Clemens took the handle of the basket. Bellermann took up a gun and Clemens looked over his shoulder at the sight. The children seemed to be happy and laughed merrily when Bellermann stuck a paper rose in Gulli's hair. They swung off to the right and I saw Bellermann counting money into Clemens' hand and Clemens' lips moving as he counted too. Then he smiled gently and looked up and thanked Bellermann.

"Come," I said to Fred as I stood up and pulled him up by his coat collar. "The children are here."

"Where are they?" he said.

We looked at one another and between us, in the foot of space that separated our eyes, floated the thousand nights in which we had made love together. Fred took his cigarette out of his mouth and said quietly, "What are we to do?"

"I don't know," I said.

He led me out into the space between the booth and an unoccupied roundabout covered with an awning of green sailcloth. We looked in silence at the tent pegs to which the guy ropes were fastened.

"Come inside here," said Fred, holding open a chink between two of the green canvas walls. He pushed through the opening and helped me in and we sat down in the half-light, Fred on a wooden swan and I beside him on a rocking horse. A ray of light, which came through the opening in the tent, fell on Fred's face and cut it in two.

Fred said, "Perhaps I ought not to have married."

"What nonsense!" I answered. "Spare me that. That's what all men say at one time or another." I looked at him and added, "Not very flattering to me, but what woman succeeds in making marriage tolerable?"

"You have succeeded better than most women," he said, raising his face from the swan's head and laying his hand on my arm. "Fifteen years have we been married and . . ."

"A wonderful marriage," I said.

"Brilliant," he said, "truly brilliant."

Then he took his hand from my arm and put both his hands on the swan's head. He laid his head on them and looked up at me sideways with a weary expression, saying, "I am sure that you are all happier without me."

"That's not true," I said; "if you only knew!"

126

"If I only knew what?"

"Fred, every day the children ask after you a dozen times and every night—almost every night—I lie in bed and cry."

"You cry?" he said and looked up again and gazed at me and I was sorry that I had told him.

"I don't say that just to tell you that I cry, but that you may know how much you are deceiving yourself."

The sun suddenly came through the opening and drenched the round green tent in its rays. In the golden light one could clearly see the animals of the roundabout —horses showing their teeth, green dragons, swans, ponies, and behind me I saw a wedding coach upholstered in red velvet and drawn by two white horses.

"Come along," I said to Fred, "we can sit more comfortably in there."

He climbed off his swan and helped me down from my rocking horse and we sat ourselves down on the soft velvet seats of the coach. The sun left the opening; we were surrounded by a circle of shadowy gray beasts.

"When you cry," said Fred, trying to put his arm round me but I would not let him, "is it because I am not there?"

"Partly," I said, "but not only for that reason. You know that I prefer you to be with us, but I realize, too, that you cannot stand it: and sometimes it is a good thing that you aren't there. Sometimes I was afraid of you. Your face frightened me when you beat the children and so did your voice, and I don't want you to come back if everything is going to be just as it was before you went away. I would much rather lie in bed and weep than know that you punish the children for the sole reason that we have no money. That is the reason why you whip the children, isn't it? Because we are poor."

"Yes," he said, "poverty has made me sick."

"Yes, and that is why it is better to stay away, unless everything changes. Perhaps in a year I shall have sunk so low that I, too, will start beating the children. Perhaps I shall turn into one of those wretched women whom it used to frighten me to look at when I was a child, a hoarsed-voiced, poor creature, driven to despair by the horror of life, living in a den in a filthy tenement block, now beating her children and now feeding them on sweets; giving herself at night to the embraces of a wretched drunkard who brings the reek of sausage booths into the house, who, when love-making is done, fishes two crumpled cigarettes out of his pocket, which they smoke together in the dark. How I used to despise such women, God forgive me! Give me another cigarette, Fred." He quickly took a pack out of his pocket and offered it to me, and by the light of the match I saw his poor face in the green twilight of the tent.

"Go on," he said, "go on telling me, please."

"Perhaps I also cry because I'm expecting."

"What, are you expecting?"

"Yes, perhaps I am. You know how I am when I am going to have a baby. I still am not sure about it, in fact I'm probably not, because, if I had been, going on the chairoplane would have made me ill. Or do you want another child?"

"No, no," he said hastily.

"But if it comes, you will have begotten it. Ah, Fred, you don't like hearing that." I was sorry that I had said it. He leaned back smoking in the coach and said, "Go on telling me, please; tell me everything that is on your mind."

"I weep, too, because the children are so quiet. They are so good. And I'm frightened by the way they go off to school as a matter of course and take school life seriously and I'm really alarmed by the trouble they take over their homework. I hear again from them the deadly chatter about classwork and I hear them using practically the same expressions as I used when I was their age. It's awful, Fred. And then the joy on their faces when they smell the little piece of meat simmering in my cooking pot, and the quiet way in which they pack their satchels in the morning, sling them over their shoulders and put pieces of bread in their pockets! And when they start for school I often slip out into the corridor and watch them as long as they are in sight. I see their thin backs bending a little under the weight of their schoolbooks as they walk side by side as far as the corner. Clemens turns off there and I can watch Carla for a bit longer as she trips into Mozart Street. She has your walk, Fred, and along she goes with her hands in the pockets of her cloak thinking about some knitting pattern or the date of Charlemagne's death. It makes me weep to see them, because their keenness reminds me of the keenness of some children who were at school with me and whom I used to hate—children who looked so like the holy children in the pictures playing round Joseph's joiner's bench—soft, attractive little creatures, ten or eleven years old, letting long shavings the color of their hair slip idly through their fingers."

"Do you mean to say that our children look like the young Jesus in the pictures of the Holy Family?"

I looked at him and said, "No, no, but when I see them walking off to school, they seem to have something in them of that hopeless, senseless humility which brings tears of rage and fear into my eyes."

"My God," said he, "but there is no sense in that. I believe that you envy them simply because they are children."

"Oh, no, Fred: I am afraid because I cannot protect them against the hardheartedness of men, exemplified by the hardheartedness of Mrs. Franke, who receives the communion every morning, but whenever one of the children has used the lavatory comes running out of her workroom into the hall to see that they have left the lavatory clean and starts scolding them if a single drop of water has fallen on her carpet. The thought of the drops of water frightens me and I break out into a sweat whenever I hear one of the children pull the plug. I can't exactly say what makes me so sad. Perhaps you know what it is."

"What makes you sad is the fact that we are poor. It is very simple and I can offer you no comfort. There's no escape from poverty. I cannot promise you that we shall ever have more money than we have now. Oh, you'd be surprised how nice it is to live in a tidy house and,

especially, to have no money worries. You'd be surprised."

"I still remember," I said, "that in my own home
everything was clean and tidy and the rent was paid
punctually and there was enough money; and when we
married, we, too, Fred, you know very well . . ."

"I know," he said quickly, "but I have very little
feeling for the past. My memory consists of a lot of holes,
great big holes patched and held together by a web of
very flimsy thread. I know, of course, that we once had
a home of our own, with a bathroom even, and enough
money to pay for everything. What was I then?"

"Fred, do you mean to say that you don't know what
you were then?"

"Really," he said, "I can't recall," and put his arm
round me.

"You were in a wallpaper factory."

"Of course," he said. "My clothes smelled of paste
and I used to bring defective catalogues home to Clemens,
who tore them to pieces in his cot. I remember now, but
that can't have lasted for long."

"Two years," I said, "until the war came."

"Of course: then the war came. Maybe it would have
been much better for you to have married some decent
chap, some steady, industrious fellow with a taste for
culture."

"Be quiet," I said.

"You would have read improving books together in
the evening—you know you like doing that—and the
children would have slept in stylishly furnished rooms.

You would have had a bust of Nefertiti on the wall and a copy of the Isenheimer Altar on a wooden background, and Van Gogh's 'Sunflowers,' naturally a high-class reproduction, over the double bed next door to a Madonna by Beuron and a recorder in a stout, red, stylish case, what? Oh, hell! That sort of thing has always bored me: elegantly furnished homes fed me up, I don't know why. What do you want anyhow?"

He asked this suddenly. I looked at him and, for the first time since I have known him, I had the feeling that he was angry. I said, "I don't know what I want," and threw my cigarette on to the wooden floor of the coach and trod it out. "I don't know what I want but I have said nothing about Nefertiti and nothing about the Isenheimer Altar, though I have nothing against them. I have said nothing about decent chaps, because I hate their guts. I can't think of anything more boring than decent chaps. Their breath stinks of decency. But I would like to know if there is anything you take seriously. You don't take anything seriously which other men do, and there are a few things which you take more seriously than other people. You haven't got a profession. You have been a dealer in medical supplies, a photographer, then you were employed in a library—it was pitiful to see you. You couldn't even hold a book properly. Then you were in a wallpaper factory, then a forwarding agency and then, in the war, you learned how to be a switchboard operator."

"Oh, shut up about the war," he said, "it bores me."

"Very well," I said. "Your whole life, our whole life,

has been spent in eating houses, where they serve sausages and goulash, in dirty public houses, in fifth-class hotels, at fun fairs, and in that squalid den which has been our home for the last eight years."

"And in churches," he said.

"Yes, all right, in churches too."

"Don't forget the cemeteries."

"I don't forget them, but never, even when we were traveling, have you shown any interest in culture."

"Culture," he said, "if you could tell me what culture is—but no, I'm not interested in it. I am interested in God, in cemeteries, in you, in sausage booths, in fairs and fifth-rate hotels."

"Don't forget the drink," I said.

"No, I didn't forget it and I will add to my list for good measure the cinema and gambling machines."

"And the children," I said.

"Yes, the children. I love them very much—more than you suspect. I really do love them. But I am nearly forty-four and I can't tell you how weary I am—think what we've been through." Then he suddenly looked at me and asked if I was cold and should we go.

"No, no," I said, "please go on telling me."

"Oh, let it alone," he said, "let us stop. What's the use of all this talk? Don't let us quarrel. You know me anyhow—you must know me well and must realize that I am a bad bargain and that at my age no one changes. I believe that no one ever changes. The only point in my favor is that I love you."

"Yes," I said, "I realize that you're no prize winner."

"Shall we go now?" he asked.

"No," I said, "let us stay here a little longer. Or are you cold?"

"No, I'm not cold, but I would like to go with you to the hotel."

"We'll go soon," I said, "but first you must tell me one or two things. Or won't you?"

"Ask me," he said.

I laid my head on his breast and was silent and we both listened to the brazen music of the orchestrion, the shrieks of the people on the chairoplane, and the gruff tones of the barker. "Fred," I said, "do you really get enough to eat? Open your mouth." I turned my head and he opened his mouth so that I could see his red, inflamed gums. I took hold of his teeth and felt how loose they were. "Pyorrhea," I said. "In a year at least you'll have to have a denture."

"Do you really think so?" he said anxiously.

Then he stroked my hair and added, "We have forgotten the children." We fell silent again and listened to the noise outside. Then I said, "Don't worry. I'm no longer anxious about the children, though I felt anxious just before. Let us leave them in peace to stroll round the fair with the young man and his girl. Nothing will happen to them. Fred," I said softly, settling my head on his chest again, "where is it you are living?"

"With the Blocks in Escher Street."

"The Blocks?" I said. "I don't know them."

"You mean to say you don't know the Blocks who lived on the floor below Father? The people who had a paper business?"

"Oh, those people," I said, "Mr. Block had such funny golden hair and never smoked. That's where you live, is it?"

"Yes, I've been there a month. I met him in a bar and he took me home when I was drunk. Since then I have been living with him."

"Have they room enough for you?"

He was silent. The tent next to us had just been opened. Somebody struck a triangle sharply several times and a hoarse voice shouted through a funnel, "Attention, please, attention. Something special for the gentlemen."

"Fred," I said, "didn't you hear me?"

"I heard you. The Blocks have room enough. They have thirteen rooms."

"Thirteen rooms?"

"Yes," he said. "Old Block is caretaker of a house which has been standing empty for three months. It belongs to an Englishman called Stripper, or something. He is a general or a gangster or both. Perhaps he is something else as well. Anyhow he has been away for three months and the Blocks have to look after the house. They have to keep the lawn in order so that it may look up to standard even in winter. Every day old Block goes over it with a roller and a lawn mower and he has to look after the garden as well. Every three days a parcel of chemical manure arrives, which he has to spread about. I tell you, it is a splendid place. There are a lot of bathrooms—four I believe—and sometimes I'm allowed to have a bath in one of them. There is a library which actually has books in it, a lot of books, and though I don't know anything about culture, I do understand

135

something about books and I can tell you that in this library there are good books, fine books, and masses of them. There is also a drawing room, if that's the name for it, and a smoking room and a dining room and a room for the dog. Upstairs there are two bedrooms, one for the gangster, or whatever he is, and the other for his wife as well as three more for guests. Of course, there is a kitchen with one, two . . ."

"Stop, Fred, do stop," I cried.

"Oh, no," he said, "I am going on. I have never told you about it, darling, because I did not want to torment you, but it is better now for you to hear the whole story. I have to talk about the house. I dream about it. Sometimes I get drunk in order to forget about it, but even when I am drunk, I can't forget it. I don't know how many rooms I have counted—eight, was it, or nine?—there are thirteen altogether. You ought to see the dog's room. It is rather bigger than ours, only a little bigger, perhaps two square yards. One must be fair. There is nothing like fairness. We must inscribe the word on our modest banner. Don't you agree, dear heart?"

"Oh, Fred, you want to torture me after all."

"I torture you! Ah, you don't understand me. But I absolutely must talk about the house. The dog's kennel is a sort of pagoda. It is as big as the sideboards usually are in these great, elegant houses. In addition to the four bathrooms there are two shower stalls which I don't count. I want to be fair. I want to get drunk on fairness. I will never count a shower stall as a room. That would be unfair and we want to write 'fairness and justice' on our modest banner. But there is worse to come, my sweet. The house is empty. How lovely the great lawns behind the villa would be if only children were allowed to play on them, or even dogs. Let us arrange to have big lawns for our dogs, dearest. But this house is empty. All the downstairs rooms are empty. On the top floor there are still three more rooms: one for the housekeeper, one for the cook, and one for the manservant. And the good lady complains because the housemaid, who must have a room too, occupies one of the guest rooms. We must think of that, darling, when we build our house, on the roof of which we shall hoist the banner of fairness and justice."

"Fred," I said, "I can't stand any more."

"Yes, you can. You have borne five children and you can stand a lot. I must finish my piece. I cannot stop. You can go away, if you like, though I would much sooner you stayed and passed the night with me, but if you won't listen to me, you can go. I have been staying in this house for a month and I have to tell you all about it, just you, though I would gladly have spared you. And I wanted to spare you, sweetheart, but you asked me and so you have to listen to the whole story. The good lady almost committed suicide because there was no servant's room for the housemaid. You can imagine what a sensitive person she is and how great her anxieties must be. Now she is abroad. They are usually away from home for about nine months in the year. The old so-and-so who lives there is an expert on Dante, one of the few outstanding Dante scholars alive today, one of the few persons in that line who has to be taken seriously. Something like our bishop as you, an educated Christian woman, will, I know, appreciate. For nine months in the year the house is empty and during all that time old Block looks after the lawn. A nice job! There is nothing more beautiful than a well-kept lawn. The dog's room must not be beeswaxed and no children are allowed in the house."

"Attention, attention," cried the hoarse voice in the nearby tent. "Something special for our gentlemen. Manuela, the loveliest creature on earth."

"Fred," I said, "why are no children allowed in the house?"

"Because the lady of the house cannot stand them. She can't bear the smell of children and she can smell them if they have been there even after three quarters of a year. Block's predecessor was an invalid who allowed his two grandchildren to play there—in the basement, of course, as is fitting—not on the lawn or anything like that. The man allowed them to play in the basement and, when the lady returned, she found out about it and he was sacked. That's why Block has to be careful. I asked him once if my children could come and visit me there and he turned as white as chalk. I am allowed to live there because I am supposed to be helping with the lawn and looking after the central heating. I have a little room downstairs off the hall. It is really a cloakroom. When I wake in the morning I look at an old Dutch picture opposite my bed—painted in soft, old colors—some sort of a tavern. There are more of these in the library. I would like to grab one of them but they would find out at once and it wouldn't be fair to Block."

"Manuela will sing of love," called the voice.

"Block thinks the lady is a queer."

"Oh, Fred, won't you stop and let us go to the hotel?"

"Only a minute longer," he said, "you must listen to me, for one minute more, and then I'll be finished and you will know where I live and how I live. The bishop often comes to the house in the evening. He is the only person who is allowed to enter the house and all the books about Dante are at his disposal. Block has been instructed to see that he is comfortable and warm and to draw the curtains. I have seen him there a few times, with a happy, peaceful expression, a book in his hand, the teapot beside him and a paper pad and pencil. His driver sits with us below in the basement and smokes his pipe. Now and then he goes out to look at the car. The bishop rings the bell when he wants to leave. Then his driver springs up and Block sees the old man to his car. The bishop calls him 'my good man' and gives him a tip—that's all," said Fred. "Now we can go, if you wish. Do you want to go?"

I shook my head because I couldn't speak. My throat was choked with sobs. I was so tired, and still the sun was shining out of doors and everything Fred had said seemed to me so false, because I had heard the hatred in his voice when he told his story. And in the tent alongside, the same voice was calling into the megaphone. "You have still time, gentlemen, to see and hear Manuela, the sweet girl who will break your hearts."

139

We heard someone climbing on to our merry-go-round on the other side. Fred looked at me. A door in the little house in the middle of the ring was opened and then shut again. The lights were turned on and suddenly the orchestrion began to play. Someone, whom we could not see, began to roll up the sides of the tent and light streamed in. A window opened in the hut in the middle of the ring and a man with a long, pale face looked at us and said, "Would the lady and gentleman like to have a ride? The first ride is free." He took his cap off and his yellow hair fell over his forehead. Then he scratched himself and, putting his cap on again, had a quiet look at me. He had a sad face although he was smiling. Then he said to Fred, "No, I don't think it would do for your wife."

"What do you say?" said Fred.

"No, nothing—" he answered. He tried to smile at me but couldn't manage it and shrugged his shoulders. Then he slammed the window to and came round the orchestrion and stopped by our coach. He was a tall chap. The sleeves of his jacket were too short and his thin muscular arms were quite white. He looked at me very closely and said, "Yes, I'm sure it wouldn't be good for your wife, but I can wait before starting up if you want to stay in the coach a little longer."

"Oh, no," I said, "we have to go."

Meantime they had rolled up the sides of the tent and a few children had climbed on to the horses and the swans. We stood up and got down out of the coach. The

140

man took his hat off, waved to us and said, "All the best, all the best."

I called back, "Thanks." Fred said nothing. We walked slowly over the fair ground without looking round us. Fred held my arm closer and led me to Mommsen Street and we picked our way through the ruins, passing the cathedral on the way toward the hotel. The streets round the railway station were still quiet and the sun still shone and its clear, bright rays showed up the dust that lay thick on the weeds covering the ruins.

Suddenly I began to feel the rhythm of the chairoplane working in me and felt I was going to be sick.

I said, "Fred, I must sit down or lie down."

I saw that he was upset. He put his arm round me and led me into the ground floor of a ruined house. Round us were high, burned-out walls. Somewhere I saw a notice saying, "X-ray clinic on the left." Fred took me through an empty doorway and sat me down on the stump of a wall and I watched him helplessly as he took his overcoat off and rolled it up. He made me lie down and pillowed my head on it. The surface under me was smooth and cool. I touched the edge of the wall with my fingers and felt the slabs. I whispered, "I shouldn't have gone on the chairoplane, but I like it so much. I can't resist a roundabout."

"Shall I go and fetch you something?" said Fred gently. "A cup of coffee, perhaps. It isn't far to the station."

"No," I said, "stay with me. Soon I shall be able to go to the hotel, but stay with me now, please."

"Yes," he said and laid his hand on my forehead. I looked at the greenish wall, spattered with red fragments from a disintegrated statue, and at an inscription which I could no longer decipher, for now my body was turning, slowly at first, like a horizontal wheel with my feet as the axle and the rest of me rotating ever faster and faster. It was like when an acrobat in a circus takes a pretty, slender girl by the ankles and swings her round him. At first I could make out the greenish wall and the white light streaming through the opening where there had been a window. The colors, green and white, alternated before my eyes but soon they ran into one another and a bright, greenish-white surface rotated round me, or I round it, at an ever-increasing speed, till I found myself wheeling round on a plane parallel with the floor in an almost colorless mist. It was only when the circular motion began to slow up that I noticed that I was lying down. But my head kept turning, turning, and sometimes seemed to be lying alongside my body and no longer connected to it, and sometimes it seemed to be lying beside my feet. Only at rare moments did it feel as if it were attached to my neck, where it belonged. My head seemed to be revolving round my body but I knew that couldn't be true. I felt for my chin with my hands and found that bony projection. Even at the moments when my head seemed to be lying by my feet, I could feel my chin. Perhaps it was only my eyes that were turning. I didn't know. The only reality for me was the feeling of sickness, when the bile rose sourly in my throat like the mercury in a thermometer and then sank sourly back.

142

It was useless to shut my eyes. When I did that I felt my breast and my legs gyrating, each in its own mad orbit, like lunatic ballet dancers, driven ever faster by my nausea.

When I kept my eyes open I could see that the section of wall always remained the same—green topped with a chocolate line and in the midst of the bright green a dark brown text which I could not read. The letters somehow seemed to shrink like the tiny letters on an oculist's test chart and then again they swelled like nasty brown sausages which expanded outward so fast that I could not grasp their form or sense, and then they burst like a splash against the wall, more illegible than ever. A moment later they began to dwindle till they were as tiny as the excrement of flies—but they were still there.

The motor which was driving me round was nausea, which was the pivot of this nightmare roundabout, and it was with a sudden shock that I realized that I was lying perfectly flat in the same place as before and that I had not moved an inch. I realized this when my nausea abated for a moment and everything became quiet and things were again related to one another. I saw my own breast and the dirty brown leather of my shoes and my eyes focused themselves on the text on the wall, which I was now able to read, "Your doctor will help you, if God helps him."

I closed my eyes but still could see the word GOD. At first it looked like writing—three dark brown capital letters visible against my closed eyelids. Then I could not distinguish the writing any more and all that remained to me was the word, which sank into my being, seemed to drop lower and lower, but found no bottom. Then it came up to the surface again at the level of my consciousness as a spoken, not a written, word: GOD.

In my sickness which drowned my heart and filled my veins, circulating within me like my blood, GOD was all that remained to me. Cold sweat broke out on me and I felt mortal fear. At moments I had thought of Fred and the children. I saw my mother's face and the faces of our lost twins just as I see them in the looking glass, but they all were swept away in this flood of nausea. I cared nothing for them all. Only the word GOD stayed with me.

I wept. I saw no more and thought no more except for that single word. The tears flowed hot and fast over my face, and from the way in which they ran down without reaching my chin, I saw that I was now lying on my side. Then once more I began to spin round, faster than before, and suddenly I lay still and leaned over the edge of the wall on which I was lying, and vomited into the dirty green weeds.

Fred held my forehead as he has so often done.

"Do you feel better?" he said.

"Yes, I'm better," I said.

He wiped my mouth carefully with his handkerchief and I said, "Only I am so tired."

"Now you'll be able to have a sleep," he said, "it is only a few steps to the hotel."

"Yes," I said, "sleep."

FRED

The natural color was returning through the pallor of her cheeks and her skin looked almost brown. The whites of her eyes, too, were deeply colored. I poured her out a mineral water and she emptied the glass. Then she took my hand and laid it on her forehead.

I asked her if I should fetch a doctor.

"Oh, no," she said, "I am all right now. It was the child. He was fighting against the curses he will inherit from us and against the poverty which awaits him."

"Fighting against the prospect of being the future customer of a druggist or a beloved member of the local clergy. But I will love him," I said softly.

145

Kate said, "Perhaps he will be a bishop, not an ordinary clergyman, or perhaps a Dante scholar."

"Oh, Kate, don't make jokes about it."

"I am not joking. Do you pretend to know what your children will become? Perhaps they will have hard hearts and build pagodas for their dogs and hate the smell of children. Perhaps the lady who cannot stand children is one of fifteen brought up in a smaller room than her dog has today."

She broke off. Outside we heard violent cracks and bangs which sounded like explosions. I ran to the window and threw it open. All the sounds remembered from the war could be heard in the flood of noise which poured into the room—the droning of airplanes, the bark of explosions. The sky, already dark gray in the twilight, was littered with snow-white parachutes sinking slowly to the ground. Each of them carried a big red flag. On the flags was written, "Griss's Rubber Goods: Protect Yourself Against the Consequences." The flock of parachutes with their banners sailed slowly down past the towers of the cathedral on to the roof of the railway station and into the streets and one could hear the jubilant voices of children who had picked up a parachute or a flag.

"What is happening?" asked Kate from the bed.

"Oh, nothing," I said, "only a publicity stunt."

And then a whole squadron of planes came storming over in deadly symmetry. They flew low over the houses, tilting their gray wings, and the sound of their engines struck fear into our hearts. I saw that Kate was beginning

146

to tremble so I ran to her bedside and held her hand.

"My God, what is this?" she asked.

We heard the machines circling over the town and then they flew away in perfect order, and the sound of their motors died away as they vanished in the distance. They left behind them a swarm of great red birds which slowly floated down into the city. The sky looked like a ragged sunset. We couldn't distinguish the balloon-birds properly till they reached the level of the housetops. Then we saw that they were storks with twisted necks and legs that dangled loosely as they fluttered down. Their loose heads hung horribly down and made one think of a company of hanged men dropping from the sky. They sailed through the gray twilight—nasty, red blobs of rubber, silent and ugly. Cries of delight rose from the children in the streets.

Kate pressed my hand without speaking. I bent over and kissed her.

"Fred," she said quietly, "I have got into debt."

"That isn't important," I said, "I owe money too."

"Much?"

"Yes, a good deal. No one will lend me any more. There is nothing more difficult than to raise fifty marks in a city of three hundred thousand inhabitants. It makes me sweat to think of it."

"Don't you still give lessons?"

"Yes, but I smoke a lot."

"Are you drinking again?"

"Yes, but not often. Since I left home I have been properly drunk only twice. Is that much?"

"No, it isn't much," she said, "I understand your drinking very well. But perhaps you could try to stop. It is so senseless. In the war you hardly drank at all."

"It was different in the war," I said. "In the war I was drunk with boredom. You can't believe that boredom makes you drunk and that as you lie in bed everything seems to be turning round. Just drink three buckets of lukewarm water and you will be drunk. That's how it is with boredom, if you are bored enough. You can't imagine how the war bored me. Often I thought about you and I telephoned to you as often as I could, just to hear your voice. That was a bitter pleasure, but the bitterness was better than being intoxicated with boredom."

"You have never told me about the war."

"It isn't worthwhile, dearest. Imagine spending the whole day at the telephone, usually hearing no voices but those of senior officers. You can't imagine how idiotic senior officers sound when they use the telephone. Their vocabulary is microscopic. I reckon that most of them do not use more than a hundred and twenty words, or, perhaps, a hundred and forty. That is too little for six years of war. Every day I had to spend eight hours at the exchange, all the time hearing such words as 'Report,' 'Action,' 'Action,' 'Report,' 'Action,' 'Last drop of blood,' 'Orders,' 'Stick it out,' 'Führer,' 'No giving way.' Then perhaps some women's gossip. And you have to imagine the barracks in which I was for three years a telephone operator. I wish I could vomit up the boredom of those years. And if I wanted to go and get tight in any place where there was drink to be had, I always ran into uniforms. I never could stand uniforms, you know that."

"Oh, yes, I know," said she.

"There was one lieutenant who used to recite Rilke to his girl through the telephone. It nearly killed me, though it was different from the usual run of things. Many people used to sing and teach each other songs on the phone, but most of them sent death down the wires. They spat death sentences into the receiver with their hard, thin voices, and the words came through to another man who had to see to it that enough soldiers were killed. When the casualties were slight the senior officers generally were of the opinion that the operation had been badly carried out. It is not for nothing that they measure the importance of an engagement by the number of the casualties. The dead weren't boring, sweetheart, or the cemeteries either."

I lay down by her on the bed and drew the counterpane over me. Below I could hear the musicians tuning their instruments, and from the bar came the sound of a man with a fine, dark voice singing a song, which was broken by the hoarse, wild tones of a woman. We could not catch the words but it seemed to be a duet with the singers singing alternately, and the rhythm was splendid. Trains were rolling into the railway station and the tones of the announcer floated through the deepening dusk like the soft murmur of a friendly voice. I asked Kate if she would like to go down and dance.

"Oh, no," she said, "it is so lovely to be able to lie quiet for once. But I should be glad if you would ring up Mrs. Baluhn and find out if everything is all right at home. And I'd like to eat something, Fred. But tell me something first. Tell me why you married me."

"On account of breakfast," I said. "I was on the lookout for someone with whom I could have breakfast every day of my life and my choice fell on you, as they say. You have been a splendid breakfast partner and I have never been bored in your company. And I hope you have never been bored with me."

"No," she said. "You have never bored me."

"But now you weep at night when you are alone. Wouldn't it be better if I came back to you, even as things are?"

She looked at me and was silent. I kissed her hands and her neck, but she turned over and looked at the wallpaper. The singing in the bar had stopped but the dance band was playing, and we heard the sound of dancing in the saloon. I lit a cigarette. Kate continued to look at the wall in silence.

"You must understand," I said quietly, "I cannot leave you alone if you are really pregnant, but I don't know if I have the strength of will to be as good-tempered as I ought to be. I love you and I hope you don't doubt me when I say so."

"I don't doubt you," said she without turning. "I promise you I don't."

I wanted to embrace her, to take her by the shoulder and turn her round to face me, but I suddenly realized that I must not do so.

"If anything happened to you again," I said, "like

what happened to you just now, you couldn't be left all alone."

"The people in the house will have a nice lot of things to say about me when they know that I am expecting a baby. You wouldn't believe how horrid it is to be pregnant. When I was expecting the little boy, Fred, you know how it was."

"I know," I said, "it was awful. It was summer and I had no money, not even a few pennies to buy you a mineral water."

"Yes, and I was so listless and indifferent," she said. "I believe I enjoyed behaving like a regular slut. I would have liked to spit on the floor in front of people."

"You even did it."

"That's right. I spat on the floor in front of Mrs. Franke's feet when she asked me in what month I was. One finds it particularly charming to be asked what month one's in."

"And that is why we didn't get the flat in the workers' building."

"No, we lost that because of your drinking."

"Do you really think so?"

"Certainly, Fred. People make allowances for a woman when she's pregnant. Oh, I know I was bad-tempered and dirty, and I know that I enjoyed being so."

"It would be nice if you could turn your head toward me. I see you so seldom."

"Oh, let me be," she said, "it is so lovely to lie like this. And like this I can think how to answer your questions."

"Well, you will now have time for that," I said, "for I'm going to fetch you something to eat and telephone to the house. Will you have something to drink as well?"

"Yes, some beer, please, Fred, and give me a cigarette."

She put her hand over her shoulder and I gave her my cigarette. Then I got up. When I went out she was still lying with her face to the wall and smoking.

The landing was full of noise and I heard the raised voices of the dancers talking to one another. As I went down the stairs I caught myself trying to keep in step with the rhythm of the dance. There was no more light on the staircase, only the same unshaded bulb. It was dark outside. In the bar there were only a few people sitting at the tables. There was another woman at the counter. She looked older than the landlady. When I came in she took off her glasses and put down her newspaper in a puddle of beer which it imbibed till it became discolored. The woman blinked at me.

"Can we have something to eat?" I asked. "We are in Number eleven."

"Do you want it in the room?"

I nodded.

"We don't do that," she said. "We take no meals up to rooms. It is slovenly to eat in one's bedroom."

"Oh," I said, "I didn't know that. But, as a matter of fact, my wife is ill."

"Ill?" she said. "That's something new. Hope it's nothing bad, nothing infectious."

"No," I said, "she's just feeling unwell."

She took the newspaper out of the pool of beer, slapped off the liquid, and put it down on the stove. Then she turned to me, shrugging her shoulders.

"Well, what do you want? There will be nothing hot for an hour."

She took a plate out of the lift behind her and went to a glass larder containing cold food. I took two cutlets and two rissoles and asked for some bread.

"Bread?" she said. "Why bread? Why don't you have salad—potato salad?"

"We would sooner have bread," I said. "It is better for my wife."

"One oughtn't to come to a hotel with a sick woman," she said; but she went to the lift and called down it, "Bread—send up a few slices of bread." A dull, angry voice came back up the lift, repeating the word "bread." The woman turned round saying, "It will take a few moments."

"I would like to telephone," I said.

"To the doctor?"

"No," I said.

She shoved the telephone across the counter. Before dialing, I said, "Two beers, please, and I'll have a schnapps now." I dialed Mrs. Baluhn's number and waited. The woman pushed a glass of schnapps over the counter and took an empty mug to the beer tap.

"Hullo," said Mrs. Baluhn on the telephone. "Hullo, who is it?"

"Bogner," I said.

"Oh, you?"

"Would you be kind enough . . . ," I began. She interrupted me, saying, "Everything is in order. I have just been upstairs. The children are very happy. They went to the fair with the young man and his girl and it's not long since they came back. They have got some balloons—red storks made of real rubber, life-size."

"Are the Frankes back already?"

"No, they won't be back till late—perhaps not till tomorrow morning."

"Then really everything is all right?"

"Yes, truly," she said, "you can be quite easy in your mind. Greetings to your wife. What do you think of her new lipstick?"

"Super," I said, "many thanks to you."

"Not at all," she said. "Good-by."

I said "Good-by," and hung up. Then I drank the schnapps and noticed that the second mug of beer was slowly filling up. The lift started to move with a growling noise and brought up a plate with four slices of bread.

I took the two mugs of beer upstairs first and put them on the chair by Kate's bed. She was still lying in the same position, staring at the wall. I said, "Everything is all right at home. The children are playing with those rubber storks."

Kate nodded and said nothing.

When I brought up the plates with the food, Kate was still lying with her face to the wall, but one of the two beer mugs was half-empty.

"I feel so thirsty," she said.

"Well, go on drinking," I said, and sat down by her

on the edge of the bed. She took two clean handkerchiefs out of her pocket and spread them out on the chair and we ate the meat and the bread off them and drank the beer.

"I must have something more to eat," she said, smiling at me. "I don't know if I am eating so much because I know that I am pregnant or because I'm really hungry."

"Go on eating, anyhow. What would you like to have?"

"Another rissole," she said, "a gherkin, and a glass of beer. Take the mug down with you." She emptied it and gave it to me. I went down to the bar again and while the woman was filling the mug at the beer tap I drank another schnapps. The woman looked at me with a friendlier expression than before, put a rissole and a gherkin on a plate, and pushed them over the wet counter. It was quite dark outside. The bar was almost empty, but a lot of noise was coming from the dance room. When I had paid I still had two marks left.

"Are you going early?"

"Yes," I said.

"Then you had better pay for the room now."

"I have already paid."

"Oh, so?" she said. "But please bring down the glasses and plates tonight. We have had some funny experiences. You'll bring them down, won't you?"

"Of course," I said.

I found Kate lying on her back smoking. "It's lovely here," she said. "What a good idea it was that we should meet in a hotel again! It's a long time since we did that. Does the room cost much?"

"Eight marks."

"Have you still got so much money?"

"I have already paid. At the moment I have only two marks left." She took her handbag and shook out the contents on the bedspread, and we sorted out the remnants of the small change I had given her at the fair from among toothbrushes, a soap case, lipstick, and some medallions. There was still four marks left.

"That's fine," I said, "we can have breakfast on that."

Kate said, "I know a nice place where we can get breakfast. It's just the other side of the subway on the left as you go from here."

I looked at her.

"It's a lovely place. There is a charming girl and an old man. The coffee is good. I still owe them for it."

"Was the idiot there too?" I asked.

She took the cigarette out of her mouth and looked at me.

"Do you often go there?" she asked.

"No, I was there this morning for the first time. Shall we go there tomorrow morning?"

"Yes," said she. She turned round again on her other side toward the window with her back to me. I wanted to hand her the plate and the mug of beer, but she said, "Not now. I'll finish it later."

I remained sitting beside her, though she had turned away from me, and sipped my beer. It was quiet in the railway station. Through the window I could see on the face of the high building behind the station a great brandy bottle picked out with electric lights which always hangs up there against the sky. In the belly of the bottle you can see the shadowy outline of a drinker and on the top of the building the ever-changing sky signs. I watched the illuminated letters flowing out of the void. I read them slowly as they came along, "Don't Be Dumb" —the words disappeared. Then tumbling out of the darkness, "Or Yet Glum." Then there was an interval of a few seconds and I felt a strange tension within me. It started again, "For Your Hang-over"—the words faded away once more and there was empty darkness for a few moments and then suddenly all the letters flared up simultaneously in the inscription, "Take Dou-lorin." Then in poisonous deep yellow, "Trust Your Druggist."

"Fred," said Kate suddenly, "I think that if we talk about the thing you wish to know, you won't get the answer you want. That is why I prefer not to talk about it. You must know what your duty is but, even if I am pregnant, I do not wish you to come home and storm around and beat the children, knowing that they don't deserve it. I don't want that. It would mean that in a short time we should be shouting at one another. That I don't want. And I cannot come to you any more." She lay with her back to me and we both stared at the sky signs which kept changing ever more quickly, more suddenly. We saw written on the backcloth of the night in every color the slogan, "Trust Your Druggist."

"Did you hear me?"

"Yes," I said, "I heard you. Why can't you come any more to me?"

"Because I'm not a whore. I have nothing against whores, Fred, but I am not one. It's horrid for me to come and lie with you somewhere in the hall of a ruined house or in a field and then to leave you and go home. I always have the ghastly feeling that you have forgotten to press five or ten marks into my hand when I get into the tram. I don't know how much these women get for what they do."

"They get much less, I believe," I said. Then I finished my beer and turned toward the wall and stared at the heart-shaped pattern of the greenish wallpaper. "That would mean that we should separate," I said.

"Yes," she said. "I think it would be better so. I don't want to put pressure on you, Fred. Knowing me, you know that, but I think it is better for us to part. The children no longer understand why you aren't with us. They believe me, it is true, when I say that you are ill, but they give the word another meaning. The children are growing up, Fred. Besides everyone in the house is chattering about you and none of them understands the truth of the situation. A lot of people believe that you have got another woman. You haven't, Fred, have you?" We were still lying back to back and it sounded to me as if she were speaking to a third person.

"No," I said, "I haven't got any other woman. You know that."

"One never knows exactly," she said. "I have sometimes wondered because I didn't know where you lived."

"I have no other woman," I repeated. "You know I have never lied to you."

She seemed to be reflecting, then she said, "No, I don't think you have ever lied to me. Anyhow I don't remember your doing so."

"There you are." I took a sip from her glass which was standing on the chair by me.

"All in all, you are comfortable enough," she said. "You drink when you want to; you go roaming about the cemeteries; when you want me you have only to ring me up and I come, and at night you sleep in the villa of the Dante scholar."

"I don't often sleep at the Blocks. Generally I find some other place to pass the night in. I can't stand the villa. It is so big and empty and beautiful and elegant. I can't bear these elegantly furnished houses."

I turned round and looked over her back at the sky signs above the high building but the same slogan about the druggist was still there. It remained the whole night, flaming up now and then in all the colors of the rainbow. We lay for a long time smoking in silence. After a while I got up and pulled the curtains but I could still read the inscription through the flimsy material.

I was greatly astonished at Kate. She had never talked to me like that. I placed my hand on her shoulder and said nothing. She remained with her back turned to me, but I heard her open her bag and then I heard the click of her lighter and saw the smoke rising above her.

I asked her if I should turn out the light. "Yes," she said, "I wish you would." I got up and switched off the

159

light and lay down again by her. She was now lying on her back and I got a shock when, wishing to lay my hand on her shoulder, I placed it on her face which was wet with tears. I tried to speak but could not say anything, so I took my hand away and felt for her firm little hand under the bedclothes and held it fast. I was glad she allowed me to do this.

"Damn it," she said into the darkness. "A man ought to know what he is doing when he marries."

"I will do everything," I said, "everything I can to enable us to get a proper home."

"Oh, be quiet," she said, and it sounded as though she were laughing. "The house is not our main problem. Did you really think it was?"

I sat up and tried to look into her face. I let go of her hand and looked at her pale face below me and saw the narrow white path through her parted hair in which I have so often buried my face. And when the letters in the sky sign flamed up I saw her face clearly in a flood of green light. She was really smiling now. I lay back again and this time she felt for my hand and clung to it.

I said, "Do you really think that that is not the crux of our troubles?"

"No," she said emphatically, "no, no. Be honest now, Fred, and tell me. If I suddenly came to you and said I had got a proper home, would you be shocked or glad?"

"Glad, of course," I answered immediately.

"You would be glad for our sakes?"

"No, I should be glad because I would be able to come back to you. Ah, how can you think . . ." It was quite dark. We lay once more back to back and from time to time I turned to see if Kate had not moved, but for nearly half an hour she lay staring silently at the window and when I turned over I saw the druggists' slogan blazing up.

From the station I could hear the friendly drone of the loud-speaker, and from the saloon below came the noise of dancing, and all the while Kate said nothing. I found it difficult to start speaking again, but suddenly I said, "Won't you at least eat something?"

"Yes," she said, "please give me the plate and turn the light on."

I got up, switched the light on, and lay down again with my back to her. I heard her eating the gherkin and the rissole. Then I handed her the mug of beer and she said, "Thank you," and I heard her drinking. I turned over on to my back and put my hand on her shoulder.

"It is really more than I can bear, Fred," she said softly, and I was glad to hear her speak again. "I understand you very well, perhaps too well. I know how you feel, and realize that you love to roll in the mud from time to time. All that I understand and perhaps it would be better if you had a wife who didn't realize it. But you forget the children. You can't ignore them. They are there, they are alive and, as things are, it is they who make our situation unbearable. You remember how it was when we had both started drinking too much. It was you who begged me to stop."

"Yes," I said, "it was terrible when we came home

smelling of drink and the children noticed it. But it was I who led you into it."

"I don't care who was to blame," she said, putting the plate away and drinking a mouthful of beer. "I don't know and shall never know whether you were to blame or not. I don't want to hurt your feelings, Fred, but I will say that I envy you."

"You . . . envy me?"

"Yes, I envy you because you aren't pregnant. When you want to, you can just buzz off and I can understand you very well. You can go walking for hours round the cemeteries and get drunk with melancholy when you have no money to buy schnapps with. You get drunk with grief at the thought of being parted from us. I know that you love the children and me too—you love us very much—but you never think that our living conditions, which are so unbearable that you have run away from them, are slowly killing us because you won't share them with us. And you won't understand that prayer is the only thing that can help. You never pray, do you?"

"Very seldom," I said. "I can't."

"One sees that, Fred, when one looks at you. You have grown old. You look like a poor old bachelor. Sleeping with one's wife now and then is not the same as being married to her. Once in the war you told me you would rather live with me in a dirty cellar than be a soldier. When you wrote that to me you were no longer a stripling: you were thirty-six years old. Sometimes I think that the war gave you a twist. You were different before."

I was very tired and everything she said made me sad

because I knew she was right. I wanted to ask her if she still loved me but I was afraid it would sound silly. I used to tell her anything that came into my mind. But now I didn't ask her if she still loved me.

I said wearily, "Maybe I have been somehow affected by the war. I am always thinking of death, Kate; it drives me absolutely crazy. In the war there were so many dead people that I never saw but only heard of. Indifferent voices quoted numbers on the telephone and the numbers were the numbers of the dead. I tried to imagine what the numbers meant and succeeded in a way in doing so. Three hundred killed meant a regular mountain of bodies. I was once for three weeks at the front, as they call it. There I saw what the dead looked like. Sometimes I had to go out at night to mend the broken lines and in the dark I often trod on dead bodies. It was so dark that I could see nothing—nothing at all. Everything was black, and I crept along the line which I held in my hand till I came to the place where it was broken. I spliced the ends of the wire together, fixed on the controller, and squatted there in the dark. When a flare went up or a gun was fired, I threw myself flat down. From there I used to speak to someone sitting in a bunker only thirty or forty yards away, but the distance seemed an eternity, I tell you, farther than the distance from God to us."

"God is not far away," she said softly.

"It was far," I said, "millions of miles from me to the voice with which I was speaking to check the connection. Then I used to creep slowly back, holding the line in my hand, knocking into bodies in the dark. I often lay down among them. Once I lay among them the whole night long. The others thought that I was dead. They searched for me and didn't find me and gave me up for lost. But I lay all through the night among the dead whom I could feel but not see. I don't know why I stayed with them, but I did, and didn't find that time passed slowly. When the others eventually found me, they thought I must have been drunk. And so I returned to the living and to boredom. You can't imagine how boring most living people are, but the dead are fine."

"You are awful, Fred," she said, but she did not let go my hand. "Give me a cigarette."

I felt for a cigarette in my pocket and gave her one. Then I struck a match and leaned over to look at her face. It seemed to me that she looked younger and better and not so sallow.

"Are you feeling all right now?" I asked her.

"Yes, quite all right," she said, "but really I feel anxious about you."

"Oh, you needn't be," I said, "the war has not broken me up. It is just as I say—I am simply bored. If you could hear what I have to hear all day long—unending, superfluous chatter."

"You ought to pray," she said, "really you ought to. Prayer is the only thing that can never be boring."

"You pray for me," I said. "Once I used to be able to pray, but I don't seem able to any longer."

"You have to go into training. You must be tough and always ready to start again. Drinking does not help."

"Sometimes when I am drunk I can pray quite well."

"Well, that's not right, Fred. Prayer is for sober people. It is like when one stands at the bottom of an escalator and is frightened to step on to it. One must keep on trying and suddenly one finds oneself on it and being carried upward. Sometimes I can see the truth clearly when I lie awake and weep, and at last all is still around me and then I perceive that I am passing the barrier. Then everything else seems unimportant—our squalor, our wretched home, our poverty, and even your absence. Nothing seems to count. We have still got to put up with our troubles for thirty or forty years, but that is not eternity. And I think that we ought to try to endure the hardships of life together. Fred, you deceive yourself with your dreaming. It is dangerous to dream. I could understand it if you had left me on account of a woman. It would have been hateful, much worse than it now is, but I could have understood it. If it had been for the sake of the girl in the coffee stall I could have understood it."

I said, "Don't speak of that, please."

"But you left me just to indulge in solitary dreams. That is not good. You like the look of the little girl in the booth, don't you?"

"Yes, I do, very much. I will often go and see her but I would never dream of leaving you for her. She is very religious."

"Religious? How do you know that?"

"Because I saw her in church. I saw how she knelt and received the blessing. I was in the church for three minutes. She was kneeling with the idiot-boy beside her and the priest blessed them both. But I could see by her attitude, her movements, how devout she is. I followed her because she touched my heart."

"What did she do?"

"She touched my heart," I said.

"Have I too touched your heart?"

"You haven't touched it, you have turned it round in my breast. I was sick for love when I fell in love with you and I was no longer young—nearly thirty—but you made my heart turn round, as they say. I love you very much."

"Have other women touched your heart?"

"Yes," I said, "quite a number have touched my heart —I don't like the expression but I don't know what else to say. I mean something gentle, not passionate. Once in Berlin I saw a woman who touched my heart. I was standing at the window of a railway carriage. A window opposite mine was let down and I found myself looking into the face of a woman who immediately touched my heart. She was tall and dark and I smiled at her. Then my train started and I leaned out and waved at her as long as I could see her. I never saw her again. Never wished to."

"But all the same she touched your heart. Tell me about all your heart-touching episodes, Fred. Did this heart-toucher wave to you?"

"Yes, she did. I must think a little, then I shall certainly remember the others. I have such a memory for faces."

"Oh, go on, Fred. Try to remember."

"My heart is often touched by children," I said, "and by old men and old women, too."

"And I have only made your heart turn round?"

"You have touched me too," I said. "Oh, dearest, don't make me use the word too often. When I think of you I am often touched. I see you going down the stairs in our block or walking all alone through the town or buying things in the shops or feeding the little boy. Then you make me feel like that."

"This girl in the coffee shop is quite nearby," she said.

"Perhaps it will be different when I see her again."

"Perhaps," she said. "Do you want some more beer?"

"Yes," I said. She handed me the glass and I emptied it. Then I got up, turned the light on, and took the empty glasses and the plate and carried them downstairs. At the counter were standing two young men who grinned at me as I put the things down. The landlady with the white, greasy face was now on duty again. She nodded to me. When I came back into our room Kate looked at me and smiled.

I turned the light out, undressed in the dark, and got into bed. "It's only ten o'clock," I said.

"Splendid," said Kate, "we can sleep for nearly ten hours."

"How long does your young man stay with the children?"

"Till shortly before eight."

"But we want to have breakfast in peace," I said.

"Will they wake us up?"

"No. I'll be awake."

"I am tired, Fred," she said, "but you might tell me a little more. Don't you know any other stories of the same kind?"

"Perhaps I might remember a few," I said.

"Go on with it, then," she said. "You are a nice man, Fred, but I would often like to smack you. I love you."

"It makes me happy to hear you say so. I was frightened to ask you if you did."

"Long ago we used to ask each other that question every three minutes."

"Yes, and for years."

"For years," she repeated.

"Come on, tell me," she said, taking my hand again and holding it fast.

"Stories about women, do you mean?"

"No," she said, "let us hear about men or children or old ladies. I don't feel quite safe with the stories of young women."

"You have nothing to fear," I said, and leaned over and kissed her on the mouth. When I lay back I found myself looking through the window at the sky sign, "Trust Your Druggist."

"Go on," she said.

"In Italy many people touched my heart—men and women, young and old, and children, too. Even rich women and rich men!"

"And just now you were saying how boring people are!"

"Now I feel different—much better—since I know

that you love me still. What dreadful things you have been saying to me!"

"I don't retract a word. Now let us go on with our game, Fred, and remember that it is a game. We can go back to serious matters afterward. And I take back nothing that I have said and the fact that I love you has no significance. You love the children, too, but you don't bother two cents about them."

"Oh, I know," I said. "You've said it all clearly enough. But now for our game. What do you choose—man, woman, or child and what country?"

"Holland," she said, "a Dutchman."

"Oh, you are mean," I said, "it isn't easy to find a Dutchman who has touched my heart. All the same I did come across such a Hollander in the war—a rich one, too. That is, he had been rich. As I was passing through Rotterdam—that was the first Blitzed city I saw: strange, isn't it, so much has happened since then that I now find an un-Blitzed city depressing—then my mind was confused by the sight of the ruins and the dead people . . ." I noticed that the grip of her hand on mine was slackening. I leaned over and saw that she was asleep. In sleep she looks very proud and rather forbidding. Her mouth is slightly open and has a sorrowful expression. I settled down, smoked another cigarette, and lay for a long time in the darkness thinking over everything. I tried to pray but could not. For a moment I thought of going downstairs once more, dancing perhaps with one of the girls from the chocolate factory, drinking another schnapps, and playing pinball machines for a while as the tables were sure to be free. But I didn't: I lay where I was. Each time that the sign on the roof of the skyscraper flamed up, it threw a light on the heart-shaped pattern of the greenish wallpaper and I could see the shadow of the lamp on the wall and the pattern printed on the blankets: bears playing ball, transformed into men playing ball, bull-necked athletes blowing enormous soap bubbles at one another. But the last thing I saw before I went to sleep was the illuminated sign, "Trust Your Druggist."

KATE

It was still dark when I woke up. I had slept deeply and as soon as I awoke I experienced a feeling of well-being. Fred was still asleep lying with his face to the wall. I could only see the back of his head and his thin neck. I got up, drew the curtain, and looked out over the railway station at the lightening gray of the morning light. Trains came in with their carriages still lit, and the smooth, full voice of the loud-speaker floated over the ruins to the hotel. One could hear the rumbling of the trains, but in the house all was silent. I was hungry. I left the window and went back to bed and waited. But I had become restless and kept thinking about the children and longing to see them and, besides, I did not know how late it was. As Fred was still asleep, it could hardly be half-past six for he is always awake by then. I was in plenty of time. I got up again, put on my coat over my nightgown, pushed my feet into my shoes, and walked quickly to the door, opened it quietly and groped along the dark, dirty corridor in search of the toilet, which I found at last in an unlit, evil-smelling corner. Fred was still asleep when I came back, I could see the lighted clocks in the station but couldn't make out what time they said. At the top of the skyscraper the sign was still blazing, sharply outlined in the gray morning light, "Trust Your Druggist." I was careful while washing not to make a noise; then I began to dress and when I turned round I saw that Fred was looking at me. He lay there thinking, then he lit a cigarette and said, "Good morning."

"Good morning," I said.

"Are you feeling quite all right now?" he asked.

"Absolutely," I said. "I feel very well."

"That's good," he said, "but what's the hurry?"

"I've got to go," I said. "I feel so uneasy."

"Aren't we going to have breakfast together first?"

"No," I said.

The hooter of the chocolate factory blew three wild blasts, tearing the morning air apart. I sat down on the edge of the bed, fastened my shoes, and felt Fred's hand in my hair at the back. He let it run gently through his fingers and said, "If everything you said to me last night is true, I shall not be seeing you again so soon as all that, so let us at least have our morning coffee together."

I said nothing, pulled up the zipper on my skirt, buttoned up my blouse, and went to the glass and combed my hair. I did not look at myself in the glass but felt my heart thumping as I fixed my hair. It was only now that I realized what I had said yesterday, but I did not want to take it back. I had felt confident that Fred would return to me, but now everything seemed unsure. I heard him get up, and saw him in the glass standing upright by the bed, and it struck me how neglected he looked. He had slept in his shirt, his hair was disheveled and his face had a morose expression as he pulled up his trousers. I passed the comb mechanically through my hair. I had never seriously considered the possibility of his leaving us alone for good, but now I did. My heart stood still, then it beat faster, and then stood still again. I watched him carefully as, with a cigarette in his mouth and a bored expression on his face, he fastened up his creased trousers, pulled the waistband tight, and then put on his socks and shoes. Then he stood and sighed and passed his hands over his forehead and his eyebrows. I could not realize that I had been married to him for fifteen years. He seemed like a stranger, this bored, indifferent contemporary of mine, who was now sitting on the bed with his head in his hands. I let my eyes sink into the mirror and thought of the promise of another life in which there should be neither marriage nor giving in marriage. That must be a fine life—no marriage, no husbands who oversleep themselves and feel for their package of cigarettes as soon as they wake up. I stopped looking into the glass, smoothed down my hair, and went to the window. I unconsciously perceived that it was no longer dark and that the sky over the station was now light gray, but I was still dreaming of that life without marriage that has been promised to us and the rhythmical words of the liturgy were running in my head. I imagined myself in the company of men to whom I was not married and who, I knew, had no desire for my embraces.

"Can I use your toothbrush?" asked Fred from the wash stand. I looked at him, said, "Yes," in a hesitating voice, and suddenly came back to earth.

"Good Lord," I said vehemently, "you might at least take off your shirt when you wash."

"Oh, what's the use?" he said, turning the collar of his shirt inward. Then he wetted a face towel and rubbed it over his face and neck and throat. The indifference of his movements irritated me.

"I will confide in my druggist," he said, "and buy myself a trustworthy toothbrush. Let us have full confidence in our druggist."

"Fred," I said sharply, "don't make bad jokes. I have never before seen you in such a good humor in the early morning."

"I am not in a good humor," he said, "or in a particularly bad one either, though it is hard to be cheerful before breakfast."

"Oh, I know you," I said. "You will find some heart-toucher to console you."

He combed his hair with my comb, paused, and then turned round and looked at me.

"I have invited you to have breakfast with me, darling," he said, "and you have not answered."

He turned away and went on combing his hair. Then he said into the looking glass, "I can't pay you the ten marks till next week."

"Oh, leave it alone," I said. "You don't have to give me all your money."

"But I would like to," he said, "and I beg you to accept it."

"Thank you, Fred," I said, "I am really grateful. If we want to have breakfast together, we had better go now."

"So you'll come with me?"

"Yes."

"Fine."

He pulled his tie along the inside of his collar, tied it, and went to the bed to fetch his overcoat. Then he burst out, "I am coming back to you. I'm certainly coming back to you and the children, but I don't want to be forced to do something which I would gladly do of my own free will."

"Fred," I said, "I don't think there is anything more to say."

"No," he said, "you are right. But it would be lovely if we could meet in another world in which I could love you as I do now without having to marry you."

"That's what I was thinking a moment ago," I said gently and could not hold back my tears. He came quickly round the bed and took me in his arms, and I heard him say, as his chin rested on my head, "It would be wonderful to see you again there. I hope you won't have a shock if I suddenly turn up in Paradise."

"Ah, Fred," I said, "think of our two little ones."

"I do," said he, "every day I think of them. You might at least give me a kiss." I raised my face and kissed him.

He let go of me and helped me into my coat. Then I packed my things in my bag, while he finished dressing.

He said, "Married people who do not love one another are happier than those who do. It is terrible to love and to be married."

"Perhaps you are right," I said.

In the corridor it was still dark and a bad smell came from the corner where the toilet was. The restaurant downstairs was closed and nobody was about. All the doors were shut and Fred hung the key of our room on a nail near the entrance to the restaurant.

The street was full of girls going to the chocolate factory. I was astonished to see how cheerful they looked; most of them were walking arm in arm and laughing together.

As we walked into the eating house beyond the subway, the cathedral clock chimed a quarter to seven. When we came in the girl was looking after the coffee machine with her back turned to us. There was only one free table. The idiot was squatting by the stove sucking his stick of candy. The room was warm and smoky. The girl smiled at me when she turned round and said, "Oh." Then she saw Fred and looked from him to me, smiled again, and ran to the free table to clean it up for us. I thought her ears were blushing with good will as she laid our places for us. But I still was restless and kept on thinking about the children and I didn't enjoy my breakfast. Fred was restless, too. I noticed that he seldom looked at the girl and stared at me when I was looking at something else, and, whenever I looked at him, he looked away. A lot of people came into the shop and the girl served them with rolls, sausages, and milk, took money, and gave change and often looked at me and smiled as if she wished to confirm our understanding—an understanding over something which, without saying anything, she seemed to take for granted. When the rush subsided she went over to her brother, wiped his mouth, and whispered his name. Then I thought of everything she had said to me the day before.

It came as a shock to me when the priest walked in—the one who had confessed me yesterday. He smiled at the girl and gave her some money in return for which she handed him a red package of cigarettes over the counter. Fred, too, looked at him nervously. The priest opened the package and looked vaguely round the room. He saw me and I saw that he was startled. He smiled no longer, put the cigarettes loose into the pocket of his black cloak, began to come across to me, then stopped, blushed, and retreated. I stood up and walked over to him.

"Good morning, Father," I said.

"Good morning," he replied, looking round with an embarrassed air. Then he whispered, "I must speak to you. I was at your house this morning."

"Good heavens!" I said.

He took a cigarette out of the pocket of his cloak and stuck it in his mouth. As he was lighting a match he said in a low voice, "You have received absolution—it is valid. I was stupid to doubt you. Forgive me."

"Many thanks," I said. "How were things at home?"

"I only spoke to an elderly lady. Was it your mother?"

"My mother!" I said in horror.

"Come and see me one day," he said and hurried out.

Fred said nothing when I came back to the table.

He had a tortured expression. I laid my hand on his arm and said softly, "Fred, I must go."

"Not yet, I must speak with you."

"I can't here: later on. My God, you had the whole night to talk to me."

"I am coming home," he whispered, "soon. Here is the money I promised to the children. Buy them something with it. Ices, perhaps, if they would like them."

He put a mark on the table. I picked it up and put it in the pocket of my coat.

"I'll pay you what I owe you later," he murmured.

"Ah, Fred," I said, "leave it alone."

"No," he said, "it hurts me to think that perhaps I have . . ."

I interrupted him and told him to ring me up.

"Will you come, if I call you?" he asked.

"Don't forget," I said, "that I still owe for a coffee and three cakes here."

"I shall remember. Have you really got to go now?"

"I must."

He stood up while I remained seated and watched him go to the counter. The girl smiled at me when Fred paid and then I got up and went with him to the door. "Mind you come back," she called and I said, "I will," and glanced at Bernard sitting huddled up, sucking the wooden holder of his stick of candy.

Fred took me to the bus. We said no more to one another. When the bus came we kissed hurriedly and I watched him standing at the bus stop, shabby and downcast, as I had often seen him before. He walked away slowly toward the station without once turning round.

I felt as if I had been away for an age as I went up the dirty staircase that leads to our home, and I remembered that I had never left the children so long alone. The building seemed restless and noisy with the sound of steaming boilers and the official cheerfulness of the radios. On the first floor Mesewitz and his wife were being rude to one another. Behind our door all was quiet. I pressed the bell three times and waited and at last, when Bellermann came to open the door, I heard the children's voices. I greeted Bellermann casually and ran by him into our room to see the children. They were sitting round the table with a decorum to which I wasn't accustomed, and when I came in they stopped talking and laughing but only for a moment. But during that moment anguish and fear took possession of me—only for a moment, but I shall not forget that moment.

Then the two elder ones got up and kissed me and I took the little boy in my arms and kissed him with the tears running down my face. Bellermann had already put on his overcoat and was standing with his hat in his hand.

"Were they good?" I asked.

"Yes, very," he said, and the children looked at him smiling.

"Wait a minute," I said. Then I put back the little boy in his chair, took my purse out of a drawer, and went out with Bellermann on to the landing. I saw Mrs. Franke's hat and Mr. Franke's cap on the hat stand and greeted Mrs. Hopf who was coming from the toilet. She had her hair in curling papers and was carrying an illustrated paper under her arm. I waited till she had gone into her room and then turned to Bellermann and said, "Fourteen, isn't it?"

"Fifteen," he said smiling.

I gave him fifteen marks and said, "And many thanks."

"Nothing to thank me for," he said.

Then he put his head inside the door of our room and said, "Bye-bye, children," and they cried, "Good-by."

I embraced them all once more, when we were alone, and looked searchingly at them but could find nothing in their faces to justify the fear I had felt. I sighed and began to cut slices of bread for them to take to school. Clemens and Carla were rummaging in their school boxes. Carla sleeps on an American camp bed which we fold up in the daytime and hang on a hook from the ceiling. Clemens sleeps on an old plush sofa which has long been too short for him. Bellermann had actually made the beds.

"Children," I said, "your father sends you his love. He has given me some money for you."

They said nothing. Then Carla came to me and took her package of bread and butter. I gazed at her. She had

Fred's dark hair and his eyes with their sudden absent look. The little boy was sitting in his chair playing. He looked at me sometimes as if he wanted to make sure that it was I; then he went on playing.

"Have you said your prayers?" I asked.

"Yes," said Carla.

"Father is coming back soon," I said, and I felt a rush of tenderness for the children. I had to make an effort to prevent myself from crying again. The children again said nothing. I looked at Carla who sat on a chair by me, turning over the pages of a lesson book and drinking her milk listlessly. Suddenly she looked at me and said quietly, "He isn't ill at all, you know. He still gives lessons."

I turned round and looked at Clemens who was sitting on his sofa with his knees up, studying an atlas. He looked at me quietly and said, "Beisem told me so. He sits by me in class."

I said, "There are illnesses which don't oblige one to go to bed."

The children said nothing. They slung on their satchels and went off and I went out on to the landing and watched them walking up the gray street, their shoulders slightly bowed under the weight of their books. The sight of them saddened me, for I saw myself going out just like them into the street with my back slightly bent under the weight of my books. I saw them no longer. I only saw myself from above—a little girl with yellow plaits thinking about a knitting pattern or the date of Charlemagne's death.

When I came back I found Mrs. Franke standing

before the mirror in the wardrobe fixing her mauve veil on her hat. The bell was ringing for eight o'clock mass. She said, "Good morning," and then came up to me in the dim hall and stood smiling in front of me before I could get back into our room. She said in friendly tones, "One hears that your husband has definitely left you. Is that so?"

"Yes, that's right," I said softly, "he has left me." I was astonished to find that I had no more feeling of hatred for her.

"He is drinking, isn't he?" She tied her veil round her shapely neck.

"Yes, he's drinking."

It was quite quiet. Inside I heard the gentle babble of my little boy talking to his bricks. Then I heard the voice of an announcer saying, "Seven thirty-nine. Perhaps you have to leave your charming wife, but maybe you still have time to listen to Bulwer's gay 'Morning March.'" I heard the "Morning March" and felt the impact of the radio's official gaiety like the strokes of a whip. Mrs. Franke stood in front of me immobile, silent, but I saw the deadly look in her eyes and suddenly I longed to hear the husky voice of the Negro which I had once heard and for which I have been listening in vain ever since—the husky voice which sang, "And He never said a mumbling word."

I said, "Good morning," to Mrs. Franke, pushed past her, and went into our room. She said nothing. I took the little boy in my arms, pressed him to me, and listened to Mrs. Franke's footsteps as she went off to mass.

FRED

The omnibus always stops in the same place. There is a sort of bay in the pavement where it has to draw up. Every time it stops there the bus gives a jolt and I wake up. I stand up and get out and, when I have crossed the street, I stop before the window of an ironmonger's shop and look at a notice which says, "Ladders of All Sizes, Three Marks Twenty per Rung." At this point I look up at the clock on the roof of the building to ascertain the right time. There is no sense in my doing this because my bus is more punctual than the clock. It arrives at precisely 7:56 A.M. and, if the clock says eight or something past eight, I know that it is wrong.

Every morning I stand for a few moments in front of the notice giving the price of ladders. Beside the notice a stepladder with three steps exhibited and, near it, since the beginning of summer, there has been a deck chair on which lolls a big, blonde woman in plastic or wax—I don't know what materials they use for making shop-window mannequins. The woman is wearing sun glasses and reading a novel called *A Holiday from Myself*. I cannot read the name of the author, which is hidden by the beard of a garden dwarf, leaning cross-wise over a fish tank. The great blonde doll lolls in the midst of coffee mills, wringers, and ladders. She has been reading her book for the last three months.

Today, however, when I got out of the bus I saw that the notice about the ladders had been changed and that the woman who had been sprawling in the garden chair for the whole summer has finished reading *A Holiday from Myself* and is now standing up on skiis wearing a blue sports costume with a flimsy scarf. Near her is a cardboard notice saying, "Start Thinking About Your Winter Sports Now."

I didn't think about winter sports, but walked into Melchior Street where I bought myself five cigarettes at the tobacco stall near the Chancery. Then I walked past the porter into the hall. The hall porter greeted me; he is one of my friends among the people who are employed in this house. He often comes upstairs to see me, smokes his pipe, and tells me the latest gossip.

I nodded to him and greeted a few of the clergy as they hurried up the steps with their brief cases in their

184

hands. At the top of the stairs I opened the door that leads into the telephone exchange. I hung up my hat and coat, threw my cigarettes on the table with my loose change, plugged in the switch, and sat down.

A feeling of ease comes over me when I sit down in the place where I work. I hear a soft buzzing in my ears and say, "Exchange," when anyone using a house telephone has dialed twice or when the red light comes on, and then I give the connection.

I counted my money lying on the table. It came to one mark twenty. Then I rang the hall porter and said, "Bogner speaking—has the paper arrived?"

"Not yet," he said, "I'll bring it up to you when it comes."

"Has anything particular happened?"

"Nothing."

"All right; I'll be seeing you."

At half-past eight I heard the attendance report which Bresgen, the head of the office, furnishes every day to Monsignor Zimmer. All the staff tremble before Zimmer, even the priests employed in the Diocesan H.Q. who have been transferred from the curing of souls to the administration. Zimmer never says "please" or "thank you," and I feel a faint thrill of fear when he dials. Every morning at precisely eight-thirty Bresgen rings. "Monsignor Zimmer." I listen in to his report. "Reported sick—Weldrich and Chaplain Huchel; absent without excuse—Chaplain Soden."

"What is the matter with Soden?"

"I have no idea, Your Reverence."

I heard a sigh from Zimmer as I often do when Soden's name is mentioned. That was the end of the first message.

The daily rush of messages does not usually start till about nine. Then inward and outward calls become frequent. There are long-distance calls which I must put through and now and then I switch myself in and listen to the conversations which, speaking generally, confirm my theory that the vocabulary of telephone users doesn't exceed a hundred and fifty words.

The word in commonest use is "careful," which constantly crops up and punctuates most conversations.

"The left-wing newspapers have attacked H.E.'s speech. Careful."

"The right-wing newspapers have ignored H.E.'s speech. Careful."

"The Christian Press has praised H.E.'s speech. Careful."

"Soden is absent without explanation. Careful."

"Bolz will be received at eleven o'clock. Careful." H.E. is the common abbreviation for His Eminence the Bishop.

The divorce judges speak to one another in Latin on the telephone when they are talking shop. I always listen to them, though I don't understand a word. They usually talk in serious tones and one does not often hear them joking together in Latin. It is odd that these two, Pütz and Monsignor Serge are the only members of the clergy employed in this establishment who show any sympathy for me. At eleven o'clock Zimmer rang up the bishop's private secretary. He said, "I must protest against the lack of taste shown by the Druggists. Careful. They have profaned, if not made a mock of, the St. Jerome Procession. Careful."

Five minutes later the bishop's private secretary rang back, saying, "His Eminence will lodge a protest privately. One of his cousins is Chairman of the Druggists' Union. Careful."

"What was the result of Bolz's audience?"

"Nothing definite as yet, but there may be news later. Careful."

Shortly afterward Monsignor Zimmer rang up Monsignor Weiner and said, "There are six transfers from the neighboring diocese."

"What sort of people?"

"Two are definitely fourth class, three low down in the third class, and one seems to be all right. Huckmann, his name is—comes of a good family."

"I know him. He's a gentleman. How was it yesterday?"

"Awful: the struggle continues."

"What do you say?"

"The fight goes on. There was again vinegar in the salad."

"But I thought . . ."

"Yes, I have been insisting on lemon juice for months. I can't bear vinegar. I call this an open declaration of war."

"Whom do you suspect?"

"W.," said Zimmer. "It must be W. The whole thing disgusts me."

"What a revolting business! We'll speak about it later."

"Yes, later."

At about eleven-fifteen Serge rang me up. "Bogner," he said, "would you like to go into the town?"

"I can't get away, Monsignor."

"I can find you a substitute for half an hour. I want you to go to the bank, if you would like to go. It might be a pleasant change for you to get out of the office for a short while."

"Who is to replace me?"

"Miss Hanke. My secretary is not here and I can't send Miss Hanke into the town because of her bad hip. Would you like to go?"

"Yes," I said.

"There you are. Well, come to me as soon as Miss Hanke arrives."

Hanke came at once. It is always a bit of a shock to me when she comes limping into my office with that curious swing of her body. She always replaces me when I am away—when I go to the dentist or go on errands for Serge who thinks that a change of occupation is good for me. Hanke is tall, thin, and dark. She developed a hip disease only three years ago, when she was twenty. I am always glad to see her soft, gentle face. She brought me some asters and put them in a vase by the window before shaking hands with me.

"Now you can go along," she said, "but tell me first, how are your children?"

"All right," I said, "they are all right." I put on my overcoat.

"Bogner," she said smiling, "someone has seen you drunk. I tell you so that you may be forewarned in case Zimmer begins to talk about it."

"I thank you," I said.

"You ought not to drink."

"I know."

"And your wife," she asked cautiously, "how is your wife?"

I buttoned up my coat, looked at her, and said, "Tell me everything. What are they saying about my wife?"

"They are saying that she is going to have another baby."

"Hell!" I said. "My wife only knows about it since yesterday."

"The secret news service knew it before your wife."

"Miss Hanke," I said, "what is happening?"

She received a call and connected it and then looked at me smiling. "Nothing special is happening," she said, "really not. People are just saying that you are drinking and that your wife is *enceinte*. Besides, you have been living apart from your wife for some time."

"Yes, of course."

"Well, Bogner, I only just wanted to warn you against Zimmer, against Bresgen, and against Miss Hecht, but at the same time I want to say that you have friends in this house, more friends than enemies."

"I don't believe it."

"Believe me, it is true," she said, "especially among

the clergy. Almost all of them like you," she smiled again, "it's the similarity in type. You aren't the only drinker."

I laughed. "Tell me something else," I said. "Who is it that is slowly killing Zimmer with drops of vinegar?"

"Don't you know?" She laughed with an expression of astonishment.

"No, I really don't."

"Good Lord, half the diocese is laughing about it, and there you are sitting in the middle of the gossip and knowing nothing about it! Dean Wupp has a sister who presides over the kitchens in the Blue Mantle of Our Lady. Need I say more?"

"Yes, go on, I know nothing about it."

Zimmer prevented Wupp from being made a monsignor. Wupp retorts by spending half a mark on a bottle of the cheapest vinegar, which is kept in a corner of the kitchen of the Blue Mantle and brought out whenever Zimmer turns up for a meal. Now go. Serge is waiting for you."

I nodded to her and went out. After a talk with Hanke I always feel a certain lightheartedness. She has the gift of divesting any subject of its gravity. Even the most damaging gossip is transformed by her into a good-natured game of Consequences to which everyone must contribute.

In the white-walled passage leading to Serge's room there are baroque figures cemented into the walls. I found Serge sitting at his desk supporting his head with his hand. He is still young, a few years younger than I, and is considered a great authority on marriage law.

"Good morning, Mr. Bogner," he said. I said, "Good morning," and went up to him. He shook my hand. He has the extraordinary gift of making me feel, when I meet him the day after he has lent me some money, that he has forgotten all about it. Perhaps he really does forget. His room is one of the few that was not destroyed in the Blitz. Its most prominent feature is a baroque faïence stove which stands in the corner. This stove is mentioned in the handbook of art monuments and the author says it was never lit because the Elector passed all his winters in a smaller castle. Serge handed me a few crossed checks and an envelope containing cash.

"It comes to sixty-two marks and eighty pfennigs," he said. "Please pay the checks and the cash into an account. You know the number."

"Yes, I know it."

"I shall be glad to be quit of the finance business," he said. "Thank goodness Witsch comes back the day after tomorrow and I shall be able to hand over to him."

He looked at me with his great, peaceful eyes and I felt that he expected me to start talking about my marriage. He was, no doubt, in a position to give me good advice. Moreover, it is natural for him to regard me as a "case" with an interesting background. In his face I see intelligence and goodness and I would like to be able to talk to him about myself, but cannot bring myself to do so. I often think that I would be ready to talk or even confess to a slovenly priest, though I know that no man is to blame for being tidy in his appearance. Least of all could I reproach Serge, whose goodness I recognize, for this quality, but, nevertheless, his spotless white collar and the perfect fit of the violet vest which shows above his soutane inhibit me from speaking to him.

I put the money and the checks in the inner pocket of my overcoat and looked up once more into his great, calm eyes which never seemed to look away from me. I saw that he wanted to help me and that he knew everything. But I saw, too, that he would not offer me help if I did not ask for it. I looked him in the face until he began to smile gently. Then I suddenly asked him a question which I had wanted to put to a priest for many years.

"Monsignor, do you believe in the resurrection of the dead?"

I looked intently at his handsome, well-groomed face and saw that no change came over it as he quietly answered, "I do."

"And do you believe," I continued, but, raising his hands, he stopped me gently saying, "I believe everything, everything about which you would like to question me. And, if I did not, I would immediately take off the robes of my profession and become a divorce lawyer. I would leave this whole heap of files lying here"—he pointed to the piled-up dossiers on his desk—"or I might burn them as they would be no use to me and no use to the people who torment themselves because they share my beliefs."

"Forgive me," I said.

192

"Oh, why?" he said gently. "You have more right to question me than I have to question you."

"Don't question me," I said.

"No," he answered, "but one day you will tell me, won't you?"

"Yes," I said, "one day I shall tell you."

I went down and picked up the newspaper in the porter's lodge and, after counting my small change once more, I wandered slowly into the town. Many things came to my mind—the children, Kate, and the things that Serge and Miss Hanke had said to me. They were perfectly right and I was wrong, but none of them knew, not even Kate, how much I longed for the children—and for her too—and there were moments when I believed that I was right and all the others wrong, just because they all spoke so well and I could never find words to express myself.

I wondered whether I should have a cup of coffee and read my newspaper. The noise of the street seemed somehow hushed though I was right in the midst of it. I heard somebody calling, "Bananas!"

I stood for a while in front of Bonneberg's window and looked at the *demi-saison* coats and the faces of the wax figures which always frighten me. I counted the checks in the inside pocket of my overcoat and made sure that the envelope with the cash in it was still there. Then my glance fell suddenly on the passage running between Bonneberg's show windows and I saw a woman whose appearance touched my heart and at the same time aroused my excitement. The woman was no longer young but she was beautiful. I saw her legs, her green coat, her shabby brown jacket, her green hat, but more than all I noticed her sad, gentle profile and for a moment—I don't know how long it was—my heart stopped beating. I saw her through two plate-glass windows. She was looking at the display of garments, but then she began to think of something else. I felt my heart begin to beat again as I looked at this woman's profile and I suddenly knew that she was Kate. Then she seemed once more to be a stranger and doubt invaded me again. I became hot all over and thought I was going crazy, but then she went on and, when I saw her directly and not through the glass, I knew that it was really Kate.

Yes, it was Kate, but she was different, quite different from the Kate I remembered. As I followed her along the street, she appeared to me now strange and now familiar—she, my wife with whom I had spent the whole of last night and to whom I had been married for fifteen years.

"Perhaps I am really going crazy," I thought.

I started when Kate went into a shop, and stopped by a barrow full of vegetables, watching the entrance, and from far away, though in fact he was standing beside me, came the voice of a man shouting, as from a distant underworld, "Cauliflowers, cauliflowers, two for a mark."

I felt stupidly afraid that she would never come out of the shop again. I kept my eyes on the entrance and looked at the grinning face of a Javanese in *papier-mâché* holding a cup of coffee in front of his gleaming teeth. I heard the voice of the vegetable seller coming up out of a deep shaft, "Cauliflowers, two for a mark," and thoughts which I couldn't grasp kept running through my brain. Then Kate came suddenly out of the shop and turned into Green Street. She was walking very fast and I was frightened when I lost sight of her for a moment. But soon she halted in front of the window of a toy shop and I was able to look at her and gaze at her sad profile and her body, which for many years had lain by me at night and which I had seen four hours ago and just now had failed to recognize.

When she turned round, I dodged quickly behind a street-vendor's stand from where I could see her without being seen; she looked into her shopping bag and fetched out a paper, while the man by me called out in a booming voice, "When you think, gentlemen, that you go on shaving for fifty years, so that your skin . . ." But Kate went on her way and I didn't stop to hear the end of the slogan. I followed my wife about forty paces behind her and crossed the tramlines which converge in Bildoner Square. Kate stopped in front of a flower-seller's stall. I saw her hands: I saw her very clearly—the woman to whom I was more closely bound than to any human being: the woman with whom I had not only slept, eaten, and conversed for ten years without interruption, but to whom I was bound by a stronger chain than cohabitation, for there had been a time when we had prayed together. I watched her buying big yellow marguerites, and white ones too. Then she walked on slowly, very slowly, in contrast to her former speed, and I knew what she was thinking of. She was saying, "I am buying meadow flowers for our children who never played in the fields."

So we moved along, one behind the other, and both thinking of our children. I had not the courage to catch her up and to speak to her. I scarcely heard the street noises which surrounded me. Far away I heard a softly throbbing voice on the loud-speaker calling, "Attention, please, attention. A special tram will start on Line H for the Pharmaceutical Exhibition—on Line H, a special tram, attention . . ."

I seemed to be swimming after Kate through gray water, no longer able to count my hurrying heartbeats, and once more I was startled when she walked into the convent church and the black leather-lined door closed behind her.

I only now discovered that the cigarette which I had lit when I stopped at the porter's lodge in the Chancery was still alight. I threw it away and opened the church door carefully, listened for a moment to the music of the organ, and then went back across the square and sat down on a bench.

I waited for a long time and tried to recall how I had felt in the morning when Kate got into the bus, but my memory wouldn't work. I felt lost and seemed to be floating idly down the stream of eternity and the only thing I could see was the black church door out of which Kate had to come.

When she really came, she seemed to be someone else. She walked faster and she had laid the flowers with their long stems on the top of her shopping bag. I had to hurry to keep up with her as she walked quickly back over the square into Green Street again. The flowers waved to the rhythm of her stride. I felt the sweat come out on the palms of my hands and staggered slightly as a painful knocking hammered at my heart.

She stopped again at Bonneberg's shop window and I was able to slip into the passage and watch her standing where I had been standing a little while before. I saw her gentle, sad profile as she looked at the selection of men's overcoats and when the doors of the shop opened I heard a loud-speaker inside calling, "Coats—at Bonneberg's. Hats—at Bonneberg's. Costumes—at Bonneberg's. Coats, jackets, or hats—everything we sell is of first quality."

Kate turned round and crossed the street. She stopped at a lemonade stall and I saw her slender hand pushing money over the counter and receiving change which she put in her purse—little gestures which I knew so well and which now wrung my heart. She poured out some lemonade into a glass and, as she drank, I heard the loud-speaker crying up Bonneberg's hats and jackets.

She slowly pushed the bottle and the glass back, took the flowers in her right hand, and once again I saw my wife go away—my wife whom I had embraced countless times—and hardly knew her. She walked fast, seemed restless, and kept turning round and I ducked and dodged to avoid being seen and I felt a pain in my heart when I lost sight of her hat.

When she came to a halt at the bus stop for Number 12 in Gersten Street, I dived into a little drink shop on the other side of the road.

"A schnapps," I said to the chubby, red-faced man in charge.

"Small or large?"

"Large," I said and saw the bus come up and Kate get in.

"Good health," said the man.

"Thanks," I said and poured the liquor down my throat.

"Will you have another?" he said with a searching look.

"No, thanks," I said. "How much does that come to?"

"Eighty pfennigs."

I put down a mark and he slowly handed me back two groschen, still looking at me intently. I went out.

I walked slowly down Gersten Street and across Moltke Square on my way to the Chancery without realizing where I was going. I passed the porter's lodge in the whitewashed hall, walked by the baroque figures, and knocked at Serge's door. As no one answered my knock, I walked in.

I stood for a time looking at Serge's writing table and at the pile of dossiers on it. I heard the telephone ring and let it ring. The sound of laughter came from the corridor and the telephone bell rang once more sharply, but I did not wake up till I heard Serge's voice behind me saying, "Back already, Bogner? You've been very quick."

"Quick?" I said, without turning round.

"Yes," he said, laughing, "you've been barely twenty minutes away," but then he came round and stood in front of me, looking at me closely, and I saw from his face what he was thinking. I was now completely awake and could read from his expression that he thought something had happened to the money. I could read it in his face.

"Bogner," he said, "are you ill or drunk?"

I took the checks out of my pocket and the envelope with the cash and handed them to Serge. He took them and laid them on his writing table without looking at them.

"Bogner," he said, "tell me what has happened."

"Nothing," I said, "nothing has happened."

"Are you feeling ill?"

"No," I said. "I am thinking of something. Something has come into my mind." And when I had spoken I saw everything once more as I looked through Serge's neat, wholesome face. I saw Kate, my wife. I heard someone calling, "Coats." Then I saw Kate again and everything I had seen as I followed her down Green Street. I saw how shabby her brown jacket was. I heard the voice announcing the special tram for the Pharmaceutical Exhibition. I saw the black church door and the long-stemmed yellow marguerites which were to lie on my children's graves. I heard someone calling, "Cauliflowers." Everything I had just seen came back to me and I could see Kate's sad, gentle profile through Serge's face.

He went out and I looked at the white wall above the stove that had never been lit and saw the *papier-mâché* face of the Javanese holding a coffee cup before his glistening teeth—the face I had seen in the shop window.

Serge came back and I heard him saying on the telephone, "A cab. I want a cab at once." Then I saw his face once more and felt money being pressed into my hand. I looked down and saw a shining new five-mark piece and Serge said, "You must go home."

"Yes," I said. "Home."